Henry Edward Manning

The glories of the Sacred Heart

Henry Edward Manning

The glories of the Sacred Heart

ISBN/EAN: 9783744737081

Printed in Europe, USA, Canada, Australia, Japan

Cover: Foto ©Andreas Hilbeck / pixelio.de

More available books at **www.hansebooks.com**

THE GLORIES

OF

THE SACRED HEART.

THE GLORIES

OF THE

SACRED HEART.

BY

HENRY EDWARD, *Manning*

CARDINAL ARCHBISHOP. *of Westminster.*

οὕτω τὸ θεῶσαν καὶ θεωθὲν εἷς Θεός.

S. GREG. NAZ. *Adv. Apollin.* Opp. tom. ii. p. 256.

τίς τοιγαροῦν οὕτως ἄφρων ἐστὶν, ὡς λέγειν τῷ Κυρίῳ, ἀπόστα ἀπὸ
τοῦ σώματος, ἵνα σε προσκυνήσω;

S. ATHAN. *Ep. ad Adelphium,* s. 3, Opp. tom. i. p. 913.

NEW YORK:

THE CATHOLIC PUBLICATION SOCIETY,

No. 9 WARREN STREET.

1875.

TO

THE STUDENTS

OF

THE SEMINARY OF S. THOMAS OF CANTERBURY,

WITH AN EARNEST PRAYER

THAT ALL WHO GO FORTH FROM ITS THRESHOLD

MAY BE APOSTLES AND EVANGELISTS

OF THE

SACRED HEART OF JESUS,

This little Book

IS

AFFECTIONATELY INSCRIBED.

PREFACE.

THE Sacred Heart is, as Simeon prophesied of Jesus Himself, 'Signum cui contradicetur.' Like the title of His Blessed Mother, who is in very truth 'Mother of God,' it has drawn to itself all the assaults of heresy. For it is a divine test of faith in the mystery of the Word made Flesh, 'ut revelentur ex multis cordibus cogitationes.' Those who had trusted with a yearning hope that the faith of Englishmen, in the Incarnation at least, was firm and clear were saddened and silenced when the pilgrimage to Paray-le-Monial elicited from some of the highest sources of the established religion a profession of simple Nestorianism.

It was then that the first fifty pages in this book were published. Having been out of print for some time, they are now reprinted, as the doctrinal foundation of all that follows.

The devotion of the Sacred Heart has two aspects : the one as the centre of all dogma; the other as the source of the deepest devotion. In this latter aspect it reveals to us the personal love of our Divine Redeemer towards each and every one for whom He died. It is a manifestation of His pity, tenderness, compassion, and mercy to sinners and to penitents. Nevertheless, its chief characteristic and its dominant note is His disappointment at the returns we make to Him for His love, and above all, His divine displeasure at the faults and sins of those who are specially consecrated to His service. He seems to be sadly upbraiding us with the three doubting questions which He put to Peter, 'Lovest thou Me?' and to be looking upon us as He turned and looked on him, when he had thrice denied his Master. Into this part of the devotion of the Sacred Heart I have not ventured. It has been already treated so profusely by others, and by many of whom I have only to learn; it is in itself so deep and so intimately related to the personal life and mind of each, that I have always felt it better to use but few suggestive words rather than to draw out devotional acts, which to the writer are no doubt spontaneous, natural, and real, but to the reader may be a burden like Saul's armour to David.

In the following pages, therefore, I have intentionally confined myself to the dogmatic side of the devotion; and for the following reasons. I believe firmly that when divine truth is fully and duly apprehended it generates devotion; that one cause of shallowness in the spiritual life is a superficial apprehension of the dogma of the Incarnation; and that one divine purpose in the institution and diffusion of the devotion of the Sacred Heart, in these last times, is to reawaken in the minds of men the consciousness of their personal relation to a Divine Master. He has foretold the dimness and the coldness of these latter days: 'The Son of Man, when He cometh, shall He find, think you, faith on the earth?'[1] 'Because iniquity hath abounded, the charity of many shall grow cold.'[2] In that day the disciples of the Sacred Heart at least will 'know whom they have believed.'

[1] S. Luke xviii. 8.   [2] S. Matt. xxiv. 12.

CONTENTS.

I.

THE DIVINE GLORY OF THE SACRED HEART.

NOTICE.

As some of the Clergy, who by their office are required to meet the objections of adversaries in respect to the Devotion of the Sacred Heart. may not have ready access to certain books, a few notes and an Appendix have been added to this Sermon.

THE DIVINE GLORY OF THE SACRED HEART.

The Word was made flesh, and dwelt amongst us; and we saw His glory, the glory as it were of the Only-begotten of the Father.   S. John i. 14.

S. John, in his first epistle, writes thus: 'Every spirit that dissolveth Jesus is not of God, and this is Antichrist, of whom you have heard. that he cometh, and he is already in the world.'[1]   The meaning of the words 'that dissolveth Jesus' is this: —whosoever denies that the Son of God is come in the flesh, that is, the truth of His Incarnation, or in any way destroys the distinction of His two natures, or the unity of His Divine Person, or denies that He is the Incarnate God, or refuses to Him divine worship and the honour which is due to God alone— whosoever in these, or in any other way, destroys or denies the truth of the Incarnation, ' dissolveth

[1] 1 S. John iv. 3.

Jesus,' and, whether he know it or not, is a disciple of Antichrist.

The Person of our Divine Lord has been, from the beginning, the centre of all the chief heresies that have tormented the Christian world. Like as in warfare, the hottest conflict is always around the person of the king, so, in the whole history of the Christian Church, the keenest assaults of heresy and the most concentrated enmity of heretics have been directed against the Incarnation of the Son of God.

In the beginning there were those who assailed His manhood, and taught that it was a phantom. Then came Apollinaris, who taught that He had a human body but not a human soul. Then came Arians, who affirmed that, if He had a Godhead, it was inferior to the Father. Then arose a cloud of semi-Arian heresies shading off in their distinctions, but all alike in denying His true Godhead. Then came Nestorius, who affirmed that He had a human person: then Monophysites, who taught that His two natures were confused into one: then Monothelites, who taught that He had only one will. For centuries the Church was tormented by a succession of heresies, all surrounding and assailing the person of the Incarnate Word, and all alike striving to 'dissolve Jesus.'

And so it has been in these later times. Three hundred years ago there was what was called a reformation of the Church of God. Among the agents of that reformation there were three who bore the most fatal sway. A hand friendly to them, thinking to glorify them in what he wrote, composed for one of them an epitaph, and it runs thus:

> ' Tota jacet Babylon, destruxit tecta Lutherus,
> Calvinus muros, sed fundamenta Socinus.'

' Babylon is utterly fallen. Luther pulled off the roof' (denying the true doctrine of our Justification); ' Calvin pulled down the walls' (denying the doctrine of the Sacraments); ' Socinus tore up the foundations' (because he denied the Incarnation of the Son of God, and therefore our redemption in His Precious Blood). These three agents of destruction have ever been at work all over what is called the Reformed Church to this day. They have been tormenting Poland and Switzerland and France—I grieve to say England in some part—and the New World, to which heresy has been carried together with Christianity. What is called Unitarianism— the denial of the doctrine of the Holy Trinity, and the denial therefore of the proper Incarnation of the Word—is the legitimate result of the Reformation. And this subtil heresy has spread widely in England,

and its coldness has spread still more widely than its formal errors. The Church which is established by law in England, so far as its books are concerned, is not indeed responsible for this. It retains the creeds, and it retains what is called the creed of S. Athanasius, in which the true and proper doctrine of the Incarnation is fully enunciated. A century ago a number of clergymen, who were at heart Unitarians, tried hard to get rid of the Athanasian Creed. In these days this effort has been renewed. Those who have authority have resisted the attempt, and I thank God for it. It is one more barrier in the way of the descent of religion —it is one more bond to hold the Christianity of England from hastening down the rapids which have wrecked the faith of Germany and Switzerland. I speak, therefore, of the Established Church of England so far with hope, and I bear a true affection to multitudes of those who are in it. I believe them to be in good faith. If they knew the light of the truth, they would give their lives for it. They would not for the world speak a syllable to derogate from the glory of the Incarnation. Therefore let nothing I am about to say be understood as reflecting on those whom I honour and love, though they be in error and in separation from the Catholic Church.

Let us, then, see what is the doctrine of the Incarnation, because, as the doctrine of the Incarnation is the true test of the disciples of Jesus Christ, so the divine glory of the Sacred Heart is the true test of the doctrine of the Incarnation.

' The Word,' that is the Eternal Son of God, ' was made flesh' without ceasing to be God. From all eternity He is God. In time He took upon Him our nature and was made man. He ' dwelt' in the midst of men, and men ' saw His glory,' and that glory was ' the glory of the Only-begotten of the Father.' It was therefore a divine glory. These are the words of the Apostle. How are we to understand this doctrine? What is the Incarnation?

1. The Athanasian Creed will tell us; it is *assumptio humanitatis in Deum* : the assumption of humanity into God. It is not the conversion of Godhead into flesh, nor the conversion of the flesh into Godhead. It is not the confusion of two natures into one. It is the assumption of human nature into the unity of the Divine Person of the Eternal Son of God. He took the nature of man ; He assumed it to Himself. And this assumption was the work of the Three Persons of the Ever-blessed Trinity, for all the works of Omnipotence *ad extra* are the works of the Father

and of the Son and of the Holy Ghost. The Father and the Holy Ghost assisted in the divine work of the Incarnation, but it was the Son of God alone who invested Himself with our humanity. The Person of the Son became incarnate, and not the Person of the Father, nor the Person of the Holy Ghost. But, as the Son of God is God, it is God who became incarnate. And in that Incarnation He assumed a human soul. In the order of reason, though not in the order of time, the Word of God assumed a human soul, and thereby a human body; a human soul like ours and a human body like ours in all its sinless infirmities; and therein He assumed the whole nature of man.[2]

---

[2] ' In which wonderful conception Wisdom built herself a house, and the Word was made flesh, and dwelt among us, and yet the Word was not converted or changed into flesh, that He should cease to be God who willed to be man; but the Word was so made flesh, that not only the Word of God and the flesh of man were there, but also the rational soul of man : and this Whole should be called God because of Godhead, and man because of manhood. In whom, the Son of God, we believe that there were two natures, one of Godhead, another of manhood, which the one person of Christ so united in Himself, that the divinity could never be separate from the humanity, nor the humanity from the divinity : nor in saying that there are two natures in the Son do we make in Him two Persons, lest, which God forbid, a quaternity should seem to enter into the Trinity. For God the Word did not assume the Person of a man, but the nature, and into the Eternal Person of His Godhead He assumed in time the substance of flesh ; so although we believe the Father, the Son, and the Holy Ghost to be of one substance,

2. The Word of God, then, so became man or incarnate, that the Person of the Eternal Son was clothed in our humanity. The countenance that gazed upon the faces of men while ' He dwelt amongst them' was the face of God; and the hands that cleansed the leper were the hands of God; the finger that opened the ear of the deaf was the finger of God; the feet that Mary kissed in her repentance were the feet of God; the hands that were bound with cords were the hands of God; the hands and the feet that were nailed upon the cross were the hands and feet of God; the Blood that was shed for the redemption of the world was the Blood of God; and the heart that was pierced upon the cross was the heart of God; because the whole humanity which the Eternal Word assumed was the humanity of God. In that sacred humanity dwelt the Person of the Eternal Son of God in all the

---

we yet do not say that the Virgin Mary bore the unity of this Trinity, but the Son alone, who alone assumed our nature into the unity of His Person. It is to be believed also that the whole Trinity wrought the incarnation of the Son of God, because the works of the Trinity are inseparable. Yet it was the Son alone who assumed the form of a servant in the singularity of His Person, not in the unity of the Divine nature, in that which is proper to the Son, not in that which is common to the Trinity: which form was fitted to Him in the unity of His Person, that is, that the Son of God and the Son of man should be one Christ.' *Symbolum Fidei Concilii Toletani*, II., A.D. 675.

fulness of His Godhead. The Son of God was not united to our manhood as the Holy Spirit of God was united to the prophets. S. Paul, in the first verse of the first chapter of the Epistle to the Hebrews, expressly says, that ' God, who at sundry times and in divers manners spoke in times past to the fathers by the prophets, last of all in these days hath spoken to us by His Son ;'[3] that is, by His Incarnate Son. Neither was the Godhead of the Son united to His manhood like as God is united to us. God is united to the soul and dwells in the soul by the indwelling of the Holy Ghost, but we are not God Incarnate. The Saints of God are perfectly united to Him and He dwells in them, but they are not the Incarnation of God. The first Adam before the fall was a man united with God, but not God manifest in the flesh. His Blessed and Immaculate Mother, though she was more closely united to Him than any other creature, because of her very substance the Son of God took the substance of our humanity and united it to His own Divine Person, yet she is not incarnate God. The hypostatic union, as it is called—the union of Godhead and manhood in one person—is distinct from this and beyond all this. The whole Godhead dwelt in Jesus, as S. Paul says, in all its fulness

<hr>

[3] Heb. i. 1.

'corporally,'[4] that is, in the body. The plenitude of Godhead dwells in the body of His humanity.

3. But, once more, there were in Jesus two distinct and perfect natures—neither changed nor confounded. It is impossible that the divine nature should become the human, or that the human should become the divine: for eternity and infinity cannot be communicated to the creature ; neither can eternity or infinity be put off or circumscribed to the outline and stature of the creature. The two natures were perfectly distinct, without diminution or confusion. They were so united that in Christ there were two intelligences. There was the divine intelligence of the Son of God, which adequately contemplates Himself and all things possible to His almighty power. There was also a human intelligence, in which was all knowledge of which the finite intelligence of man is capable. And, as there were two intelligences, so I may say there were also two hearts; for the Holy Ghost, writing of the perfections of God, has used the language of man. In the book of Genesis we read: 'That when the Lord beheld the wickedness of man upon earth He was touched with sorrow of heart ;'[5] and when the Holy Ghost would describe the perfections of David, and the love

<hr>

[4] Col. ii. 9, σωματικῶς.   [5] Gen. vi. 5, 6.

that God had for him, He described him as 'a man after God's own heart.'[6] The love and the sanctity of God are here spoken of under the symbol of a heart. And this, I may say, is the eternal heart of God. But the heart of Jesus is a heart of flesh—a heart taken from the substance of His Blessed Mother —a symbol, indeed, because it best symbolises and manifests the eternal love of God; but it is more than this, it is also a reality.   And that human heart of Jesus was, in the hypostatic union, united with the eternal charity and sanctity of God—all the ardour of the eternal love was there, and all the fervour and all the tenderness of our humanity was there.   And as He had two hearts, He had also two wills.[7] There was in Him from all eternity the divine will, which is the love and wisdom of God acting in the absolute har- mony of their perfections.   And there was also a human will like our own—the spring and origin of all our actions.   And these two wills were so per- fectly conformed to each other—like two notes in harmony—so identical and yet so distinct, that there

[6] Acts xiii. 22.

[7] 'Wherefore, as we confess Him to have two natures, that is Godhead and Manhood, neither confounded, nor divided, nor inter- changed; so the rule of piety teaches us that He, one and the same, our Lord Jesus Christ, had also two natural wills and two natural operations, as being perfect God and perfect man.' *Epistola Agathonis et Romanæ Synodi ad Concil. Œcum. VI.*

never was, and never could be, a variation or a shadow of conflict between them.[8]   The Son of God from all eternity willed this great mystery of His Incarnation; and in time, by the spirit of prophecy, He said, 'In the head of the book it is written of Me—*Ecce venio*—Behold, I come to do Thy Will, O God.'[9]   When He came into the world He said, 'My meat is to do the

---

[8] ' And that in Him were two natural wills or volitions, and two natural operations without division, or change, or separation, or confusion, ... and two natural wills not contrary, God forbid, as impious heretics have said, but His human will subjected to His Divine and Almighty Will without resistance or reluctance.   For the will of the flesh must needs be moved and subjected to His Divine will, according to the doctrine of Athanasius, who was most wise : for as His flesh is called and is the flesh of God ($\sigma\grave{\alpha}\rho\xi$ $\tauο\hat{υ}$ $\Theta\epsilon ο\hat{υ}$), so also the natural will of His flesh is called and is the will of God, according to His own declaration, " I came down from heaven, not that I should do My own will, but the will of Him that sent Me," that is, the Father.   He called the will of the flesh His own Will, as also His flesh became His own; for as the most holy and spotless and living flesh being deified was not destroyed, but remained in its own state and kind, so also His human will being deified was not destroyed, but was rather preserved, according to the saying of Gregory Theologus : " For His will, which is understood, in the Saviour is not contrary to God, but is wholly deified. We adore also two natural operations without division, without change, without separation, without confusion in Him our Lord Jesus Christ, our true God, that is, the divine operation and the human operation; as the divine teacher Leo most clearly asserted, for each nature wrought that which was proper to itself in union with the other; the Word, that is, operating that which is of the Word, and the body accomplishing that which is of the body." ' *Definitio Synodi VI.* Const. III. A.D. 680.

[9] Ps. xxxix. 8.

will of Him that sent Me.'[10] In His agony in the garden He said, 'Father, if it be possible, let this chalice pass from Me; nevertheless not My will, but Thine be done.'[11] There was then no conflict in His human will. It was in perfect conformity with the divine.   And upon the cross He offered Himself; as the prophet Isaias wrote, '*Oblatus est quia ipse voluit*[12]—He offered Himself because He willed it.' Of His own will He gave up the Ghost: 'Father, into Thy hands I commend My Spirit.'[13] And these free acts of our Divine Redeemer had an infinite merit.   It was the free oblation of the life and of the Blood of God that redeemed the world.

4. But though He had two natures, two intelligences, two hearts, and two wills perfect and distinct, yet there was but one agent.   All His actions were divine and human, because the agent is both God and man.   His actions are therefore called *theandric* or *deiviriles*, because they are the actions of God and man.   There is but one agent, because there is but one person; and that one person is the Person of the Eternal Word.   In the Incarnate Son there is no human personality, neither could there be.   For a person is a rational nature, complete and

[10] S. John iv. 34,   [11] S. Mark xiv. 36.
[12] Isaias liii. 7.   [13] S. Luke xxiii. 46.

perfect, subsisting in itself, independent of all others. The Eternal Son of God is a person complete and perfect in Himself; therefore a human person in Jesus there could not be.[14] If there had been a human person, Jesus could not have been God Incarnate. He might have been the son of a woman, and therefore the son of man, but He would not have been the Incarnate God. And it was impossible that there should be confusion in His personality, for, as I said before, a human person cannot become a divine person; because he cannot cease to be finite; and a divine person cannot become a human person, because he cannot cease to be infinite. Two persons cannot coexist without real distinction. And if there had been a human personality, Mary would have been, as Nestorius said, Mother of Christ, not Mother of God. Therefore, the Person of the Eternal Son was the sole and only personality in our Redeemer. In assuming our humanity, there was never a moment of time when that human nature existed

[14] 'Uniri hypostaticè Deum et hominem, nihil esse aliud quam naturam humanam non habere propriam subsistentiam, sed assumptam esse a Verbo æterno ad ipsam Verbi subsistentiam.' Bellarm. *De Incarn.* lib. iii. c. viii. 3.

'Hoc est, unionem hypostaticam consistere in communicatione subsistentiæ Verbi non in communicatione attributorum Deitatis.' Ibid. s. 15.

separate from or independent of the personality of the Eternal Son of God.   The act of the Incarnation was an instantaneous act of almighty power.   The Eternal Son clothed His Person with our manhood, and thereby anticipated all human personality by His own.   If that human nature had ever for one moment subsisted independently, it would have had its own personality.   But it was never for one moment conceived independent; and cannot, even in thought, be separated from the Person of the Eternal Son without ceasing to be the Humanity of God.   The absence of human personality in the Incarnation of the Son is no imperfection of the Sacred Humanity. It is its highest perfection.   Our human nature was elevated; it was perfected with a perfection above its own, and was thereby lifted above the order of creation.   It was assumed into immediate union with a divine Person, and because it was assumed into the unity of a divine Person it was in Him united to the Divine Nature, and thereby deified.   It became the flesh of God—it became from that moment unto all eternity the flesh of God, because those two natures subsisting in the Eternal Word can never be divided. And at the right hand of God there sits the Incarnate Son; God clothed in our humanity for ever.   As, then, there never was a moment when His sacred humanity was separated from the Person of the Eternal Son, so there never shall be.

5. Lastly, as I have said, the humanity of Jesus, being the humanity of God, was thereby *ipso facto, eo ipso,* in the very moment of the Incarnation, by necessity, deified, for it became the flesh or the humanity of God.[15] Now there are two senses in

[15] S. Athanasius says: 'God Himself was made Flesh that His Flesh might be made God the Word.' *Lib. de Human. Natura Suscepta.* sect. 3, tom. ii. p. 873, ed. Ben.

'Therefore he assumed a human and ingenerate body that, having renewed it as its maker, He might make it God,' *i.e.* 'deify it.' *Orat. II. contra Arianos,* 70, tom. ii. p. 537.

'Though the Flesh regarded in itself be a part of things created, yet it has been made the Body of God.' *Ep. ad Adelphium,* sect. 3, *S. Ath. Opp.* tom. ii. p. 912.

'He deified that which He put on.' *Orat. contra Arianos,* i. s. 7.

'The Lord when made man for us, and bearing a body, was no less God, ... but (He) rather deified it.' *Ep. in Defence of the Nicene Creed,* sect. 3.

'For He received it as far as man's nature was exalted ; which exaltation was its being deified.' *Orat. I. contra Arianos,* s. 45.

'Being God, He has taken to Him the flesh, and being in the flesh makes the flesh God, θεοποιεῖ; *i.e.* He deifies it.' *Orat. III. contra Arianos,* sect. 38.

S. Cyril of Alexandria says: 'We never say that the flesh of the Word was made divinity, but divine, forasmuch as it was His own (flesh). For if the flesh of man is called human, what hinders our calling that (flesh) divine which is the flesh of God the Word ? Why then mock and revile the apotheosis of that holy flesh which we rightly understand to be deification?' *S. Cyrill. adv. Nest.* ii. 8, tom. vi. p. 51.

Again he says: 'Therefore we assert the Body of Christ to be divine; since it is the Body of God, adorned with ineffable glory, incorruptible, holy, life-giving; but that it has been changed int

which the Fathers and theologians of the Church in speaking of Jesus use the word 'deified.' The one is that which I have already affirmed; and that is the proper, definite, and original sense of the word, namely, that the humanity which Jesus assumed is the humanity of God Himself. The other sense is, that being the humanity of God, it was altogether pervaded by the presence and by the communicable perfections of God. The Fathers liken it to the iron which, glowing with fire, is pervaded by the nature of fire; so the whole humanity of Jesus was pervaded by the personal presence and sanctity of the Son of

---

the nature of deity neither any of the holy Fathers either thought or said; nor do we so think.' S. Cyrill. tom. v. p. 139.

S. John Damascene also writes as follows: 'The Word Himself was made flesh, conceived of a Virgin and manifested to be God with the nature He assumed, which was already deified by Him in the moment when it began to exist. So that there were three things simultaneous—"Assumption, Existence, Deification."' He calls the Blessed Virgin Mother of God, 'propter deificationem humanitatis.' S. Joan. Damasc. *De Fide Orthodoxa*, iii. 12.

S. Thomas says (Part III. q. ii. art. 1):

'As S. John Damascene says: "The Divine Nature is said to be incarnate because it is personally (*hypostaticè*) united to the flesh, not that it is converted into flesh. In like manner the flesh is said to be deified (as he also says), not by conversion, but by union with the Word, without change in its natural properties, so that the flesh is understood to be deified because it is made the flesh of God the Word, not because it is made (to be) God."'

Also in q. xvi. art. 3, S. Thomas says:

'And in this manner the human nature is not called essentially

God. It had, as the Fathers say, a twofold unction, whereby He was anointed as the Christ. It has the uncreated sanctity of the Son, and the created sanctification of the Holy Ghost. But this is a secondary sense derived from the true and proper meaning of the word 'deify,' which is that our humanity in Him became the humanity of God.

Now, if any man does not hold this truth, he does not hold the doctrine of the Incarnation. He may think he does. He may intend to do so. He may deceive himself; he may deceive others. But he does not hold the doctrine of the Incarnation as

---

God (Deus), but deified; not indeed by conversion of it into the divine nature, but by union with the divine nature in one Person, as is evident from Damascene (*De Fide Orthod.* lib. iii. c. xi. xiii.).'

And again (q. xvi. art. 5), S. Thomas says :

' Both natures in Christ are united to each other in the Person, by reason of which union the divine nature is said to be incarnate, and the human nature to be deified.'

De Lugo teaches as follows :

' Though,' he says, ' the Deity be not united immediately with the humanity, but only mediately (*i.e. mediante Persona*), yet this is enough, that it should truly deify the humanity. For the Deity alone, and not the Personality, is (*forma deificans*) that which deifies the humanity.' *De Incarn.* disp. xvi. sect. 1, 39.

The sixth Œcumenical Council says : ' As His holy spotless animate flesh (*i.e.* with the soul) was not destroyed by being deified, but remained in its own state and nature, so also His human will being deified was not destroyed.' This use, then, of the term ' *deify*' is consecrated in a definition of faith.

delivered by the Holy Ghost, as taught to the world by the Apostles, as defined by the Church of God, and as it is the doctrine of divine and Catholic Faith necessary to all who hope for salvation. But if the Sacred Humanity be the humanity of God, then it is invested with all the divine glories. As our Lord Himself has said, 'And now, Father, glorify Me, with the glory that I had with Thee before the world was.'[16] 'Before the world was.' What, then, is this glory but the divine? What was the glory of Jesus before the world was, but the glory which He had with the Father as the Eternal Word? Therefore, the humanity of Jesus is glorified with the divine glory in all its fulness. He was exalted to the right hand of God to sit in the glory of the Father, to be adored and worshipped in one divine glory with the Father and the Holy Ghost.

He is the Divine High-Priest by whom the world is redeemed. If the body on the cross had not been the body of God, God could not have given His life for us. But S. John writes by the Holy Ghost, 'In this we have known the charity of God, because He hath laid down His life for us.'[17] What life did God lay down upon the cross, if the sacred humanity and the life thereof was not the life of God? And if the Blood

[16] 1 S. John xvii. 5.   [17] Ibid. iii. 16.

that was shed on the cross was not the Blood of God,
how was the world redeemed ?   Your blood and my
blood, even though we were saints, would not redeem
even ourselves from our own sins, much less redeem
the world.   What, then, is the Blood which redeemed
the world?   What is the Blood which is offered for
ever for us before the mercy-seat in the glory of the
Father?   It is the Precious Blood of God the Son,
the Eternal Word Incarnate.   And at the right
hand of the Eternal Father He offers perpetually
His own Divine and Adorable Blood, which is the
Blood of God, for the propitiation of the sin of the
world.

Therefore He is also to be worshipped as the
Judge who shall judge the living and the dead.   He
who will come again is to be adored as the Creator
and Redeemer and Judge of all mankind.   And He
sits there in all the royalties of His Father's Kingdom.
'All power in heaven and on earth is given unto Me;'
and He is adored there both as God and man in the
glory of the Ever-blessed Trinity.   And as He is to be
adored with divine worship at the right hand of the
Father, so He is to be adored upon the altar present
in the Blessed Sacrament.   And wheresoever He is
adored in heaven or on earth, His Sacred Heart is
adored with divine worship.   For the Sacred Heart

is the Heart of God the Son, the true and proper Object of divine adoration and of divine worship. If this be not so, what is it that we say, day by day, at the altar, what have we been saying now in the 'Gloria in excelsis:' 'Thou only art holy, Thou only art the Lord, Thou only, O Christ Jesus, art most high in the glory of God the Father'? 'For which cause God also hath exalted Him, and hath given Him a name which is above all names; that in the name of Jesus every knee shall bow, of those that are in heaven, on earth, and under the earth: and that every tongue should confess that the Lord Jesus Christ is in the glory of God the Father.'[18] What is this worship but divine worship? What is this glory but divine glory? What is this but the very words of the Evangelist?—'The Word was made flesh, and dwelt among us; and we saw His glory, the glory as it were of the Only-begotten of the Father' in the depths and the splendours of the uncreated light of the Father and of the Son and of the Holy Ghost.

I have drawn out this doctrine, so far as time permits, in greater fulness, not without a purpose. At the outset I said that the doctrine of the Incarnation is the test of the true disciples of Jesus

[18] Phil. ii. 9-11.

Christ. The Apostles who conversed with Him, and then preached His Incarnation to the world, were the witnesses that God was come in the flesh. They declared His divine glory. The test of their true discipleship was their fidelity to this truth, which is His very Person. So is it with us. And as the Incarnation is the test of our true discipleship, the divine worship and glory of the Sacred Heart is the test of our true faith in the doctrine of the Incarnation. Any man who denies this, or even a shadow of its perfect truth—any man who, by subtil distinctions, attempts to deprive the Sacred Heart of divine worship and glory—thereby convicts himself of heresy.[19] Whether it be only material or whether it

[19] 'But, you say again, we do not give adoration to a creature. O, fools, why do you not understand that the body of the Lord which was made does not receive the adoration of a creature, for it is become the body of the uncreated Word, and to Him whose body it is become you offer your worship. It is therefore adored as it ought to be, and it is divinely adored, for the Word is God, whose own body it is. Wherefore when the women approached the Lord, He hindered them, and said, "Touch Me not, for I am not yet ascended to My Father." .... And yet approaching Him they held His feet, and adored Him. They held the feet and adored God, feet having bones and flesh that might be touched, but being the feet of God they adored God: and, in another place, the Lord said, "Touch Me, and see, that a spirit hath not flesh and bones, as ye see Me to have." ' *S. Athanasii contra Apollin.* lib. i. sect. 6, tom. i. p. 926, ed. Bened.

Again he says : 'Who is there so mad as to say, "Stand apart

be formal heresy, I do not say, for I cannot read the heart; but a heretic such man is, for he denies a divine truth, and that the highest truth in the hierarchy of faith.   As it was after the time of the Council of Ephesus, when the title 'Mother of God' was the test of the true doctrine of the faith, and a confession that in Jesus there was one only person and that person divine, so that any man who refused to give to the Mother of Jesus the title of Mother of God thereby convicted himself of heresy, so is it now, in these days, with the worship of the Sacred Heart.   Any man who denies to the Sacred Heart divine glory and divine worship, thereby convicts himself of heresy.   And do not think that this is a heresy of the imagination, verbal and unreal.   No, it is here, floating round about in the air we breathe.   It pervades multitudes who profess to believe in the Incarnation. The Jansenists, two centuries ago, set the example on

---

from the body, that I may worship thee." ' *Ep. ad Adelphium,* sect. 3, tom. i. p. 913.

S. Thomas (p. iii. q. xxv. art. 1) : ' Is the Divinity of Christ and His Humanity to be adored by one and the same adoration ?'

He quotes the Fifth General Council, canon ix., and affirms that the Divinity and Humanity of Christ are to be adored with one and the same adoration.

In art. 2 he asks whether the Humanity of Christ is to be adored with the adoration of latria.   He answers that the Humanity of Christ is to be adored with latria.

the first rise of the devotion of the Sacred Heart. They accused those who adored it of separating the Sacred Humanity. For manifold errors they were condemned by the Bull *Unigenitus*, and exist no longer. Afterwards the Synod of Pistoia, following in their footsteps, accused those who adored the Sacred Heart of separating the human nature of Jesus from the divine. They, too, were condemned by the Bull *Auctorem Fidei*, for uttering on this head an opinion 'false, scandalous, and injurious' to those who adore the Sacred Heart of Jesus. They, too, have passed away. In these days we have heard the same things once more. Old errors come up again, and spread from mouth to mouth. They are at this moment busy and malicious. Not in the hearts of the great English people; I bear them witness. The last time I spoke to you on this subject was to give a benediction to those who went on a pilgrimage of devotion in honour of the Sacred Heart; and I bear honourable witness to the public opinion of England, that though there were many strange sounds and some uncouth and sharp sayings from the tongues and the pens of men, yet in the main the utterance of the English mind, as we read it daily, was full, perhaps, of a perplexed wonder, but also of a true reverence, partly out of respect for honest men fearless in confessing their faith, partly out of a manly reverence for a sacred subject, and, perhaps, too, out of a consciousness half-suppressed that they did not comprehend it as fully as they ought. I have seen nothing that has impressed me more with a belief of the religious character of the English people than the way in which, during those days, I may say weeks, this sacred subject was handled in daily discussion. For the most part it was treated with respect. Here and there, indeed, forked lightnings came through the clouds of mental darkness, and certain sounds of ignorance and of impiety. But they were not enough to qualify what I have said. What I add, therefore, I confine to a handful of individuals. They are few in number and of little power, but of a strange malice. It is indeed very strange, brethren, that there should be men who delight in evil, who exult over a heresy whensoever they hope they can find it. It is to them a revel if they can impute error or evil to what they call the Roman Church. A Catholic delights in the truth, and every particle of truth that he can find in any of those who are separated from the Church he accepts with joy. He blesses God for it. He has so much the more in those who are separated from him. He is so much the more united to them, because they are more united to the truth. Not so those who are out both of truth and of charity. They will find evil if they can with joy, and impute it where it cannot be found. But the man that rejoices in the hope that any fellow Christian, to say nothing of any Christian teacher, should depart even a hair's-breadth from the truth, such a man is doing the works of one whom he would not acknowledge to be his father. His inspiration is not of God. Such malice is not the malice of mere nature. There remains but one other source of inspiration.

Therefore, brethren, if you are called 'worshippers of men,' or 'worshippers of flesh,' which are the two titles given by the Arians and the Nestorians to the Catholics of old, do not be alarmed. We have been called harder things than these. We have been called 'worshippers of bread,' because we adore Jesus in the Blessed Sacrament, and we have been called 'worshippers of Mary,' though the very syllables convict our modern Nestorians of false witness. They well know that no one gives divine honour to the Mother of God; but every true disciple of Jesus gives divine worship to the Sacred Heart of her Son. Do not be afraid, then, if you are assailed for His sake. Is it not a grace?

Is it not a dignity?   Is it not a happiness to be
reviled for the divine worship of the Sacred Heart?
It will not harm you.   It will not divide you from
Him.   It will only bind you closer to Him and Him
to you.   Could you be irritated by an accusation so
grateful to Him?   No; rather thank God for it.
'If you be reproached for the name of Christ, you
shall be blessed: for that which is of the honour,
glory, and power of God, and that which is of His
Spirit, resteth upon you.[20]   The Sacred Heart will
be to you a covert from the storm and a shelter
from the wind, and as 'rivers of water in drought,
and as the shadow of a rock standing out in a desert
land.'[21]   Enter, then, into the Sacred Heart, and all
these things will pass by you as the harmless wind.

One word more I must say before I conclude.
It is a great glory to the Catholic Church in England
to stand out almost alone in the broad light of day,
and in the face of the English people, as the witness
for the full and explicit faith of the Incarnation; as
the witness for the Sacred Heart of Jesus; as the
witness of its love and of its tenderness, and of the
one Name by which alone we can be saved.   To be
the full, explicit, and inflexible witness for all these
divine things—for the Person of Jesus, for the sole

[20] 1 S. Peter iv. 4.   [21] Isaias xxxii. 2.

divine personality of the Incarnate Son, for the dignity of His Immaculate Mother, and for the sympathy and tenderness of His Sacred Heart—to be the witness for all this is a joy and a glory. England has to make a reparation. The doctrine of the Incarnation, as I have said, is indeed in the heart of the English people. But it is gravely threatened, and in every generation that passes I fear its light is becoming fainter and fainter, and the faith of men in that mystery is growing less and less. And why? Because the divine defences of that truth have been ruined in England. There are two outworks of the faith of the Incarnation. Like as we see in warfare, the outworks which defend the citadel must be taken before the citadel can be assailed. So it is with the Faith. The two outworks which protect the Incarnation are the worship or devotion which we give to the Blessed Mother of God and the divine adoration of Jesus in the Most Holy Sacrament. Three hundred years ago the very name of the Mother of God was cast out. Her chapels were ruined, her festivals were abolished, her rosary was taken from her children. Every memorial of her was effaced. The little ones of England who had been trained up till then with her beads in their hands were thenceforward to know nothing of her as their Mother. Too effectually has this work been done. But more than this: the altars were pulled down. The very name of sacrifice was effaced. The festivals in honour of the Blessed Sacrament were abolished. The word priest—everything that told of the Holy Mass, everything that manifested the presence of Jesus on the altar, the tabernacle and the light that burnt before it—all these things were taken away. And when these two outworks were destroyed, the citadel itself was assailed. The doctrine of the Incarnation has been battered ever since, and to this day its light has been fading in England.

And therefore I believe that the work of grace which God has revived in the midst of us in these days is a providential warning. I believe that this restoration of the light of the Sacred Heart, come whence it may, and I know not whence it came, has been ordained to revive with an intense fervour and with a sevenfold ardour our devotion to the Person, the Name, the Passion of our Divine Redeemer. It is come to restore the faith of England—first, in the Incarnation; secondly, in the presence of Jesus upon the altar; thirdly, in a joyful recognition that the title of Mother of God is truly the right of her who bore into this world the Divine Infant, God the Son Incarnate.

A great grace, then, has been poured out upon us and upon the people of England, and there will come a time, hastened by these things, when thousands and ten thousands of hearts will return again to the true Mother of their faith. I believe that in the confusions we hear around us the announcement may be heard that the light of the Incarnation will spread once more over England in renewed splendours from sea to sea.

But, dear brethren, in the midst of this visitation of Grace let us not be without a holy fear.   If Jesus be now among us, He has come to put us on our trial: 'His fan is in His hand, and He will thoroughly purge His floor, and gather the wheat into His garner, and the chaff He will burn up with unquenchable fire.'[22]

[22] S. Matt. iii. 12.

APPENDIX I.

THE DEIFICATION OF THE SACRED HUMANITY.

Though the proofs from Fathers, Schoolmen, Theologians, and Councils already given in the notes be fully sufficient, the following may be of use, as they show how the doctrine and terminology of the Deification of the Sacred Humanity pervades Theology.

Petavius says: 'That humanity is assumed by God is nothing else but that it is *deified.*'[1]

Franzelin also writes: 'In the human nature, Incarnation is the being so united that the humanity subsists not in itself but as a nature of the Word in the Word, which is properly that which is called by the Fathers the deification of the human nature.'[2]

S. John Damascene writes as follows:

'It is necessary, then, that we should know that the flesh of the Lord is deified, and, moreover, is called God and becomes God, as Gregory Theologus says (speaking of the two natures), " of which one deified and the other was deified," and I am bold to say, is partaker of the same deity. The Anointer

---

[1] *Petav. de Incarn.* lib. iv. c. ix.
[2] *De Verbo Incarn.* p. 290.

became man, and the Anointed, God; and this not by change of nature, but according to the economic, that is, the hypostatic union, by which (humanity) was indissolubly united with God the Word, and the two natures mutually embraced each other, as we say of fire when it pervades iron: for as we confess the incarnation (of God) without change or conversion, so also we affirm of the deification of the flesh. For neither because the Word was made flesh did it pass beyond the bounds of its own Godhead, nor of its own proper and divine perfections; nor, indeed, did the deified flesh depart from its own nature or from its natural properties: for after their union the natures were unconfounded and the properties of each were inviolate: but the flesh of the Lord was enriched with divine operations by reason of its most pure hypostatic union with the Word, for the flesh by no means forfeited its natural properties, nor from its own energy did it exercise divine operations, but through the Word who was united with it, and through it manifesting His own power. For the glowing iron does not possess the power of burning by reason of its own nature, but by reason of its union with fire.

'For the flesh, which was mortal in itself, was life-giving by reason of its hypostatic union with the Word. In like manner we affirm the deification of the will, not as if its natural movement were changed, but because it was united to the Divine and Almighty Will, and became the Will of God made man. Wherefore, when it would conceal itself it was not able of itself: forasmuch as the Word of God was pleased to manifest the infirmity of the human will truly existing in Himself; and again by His Will He cleansed the leper by reason of the union of the (human) with the divine. We must know, then, that the deification of the nature and of the will declares emphatically and demonstratively the two natures and the two wills, as the glowing of fire does not change the nature of that which is heated by it into the nature of fire, but manifests both that which is ignited, and that which ignites, and shows them to be not one but two, so the deification does not make up one compound nature but contains the two (natures), and the hypostatic union : for Gregory Theologus declares one of the two natures deifics and the other is deified, for in saying " of which" and " the one and the other," he demonstrates that they are two."[3]

De Lugo writes thus : ' The Deity is the same in the Father and the Son, yet it is not the Father that

---

[3] *De Fide Orthod.* lib. iii. c. xvii. tom. i. p. 239. See also lib. iii. c. xii. p. 224, and lib. iv. c. xviii.

formally deifies or sanctifies the humanity, but the Son, because the Deity as it is in the Son, and not as it is in the Father, has the *condition* necessary for that effect, that is to say, the Subsistence (hypostasis) of the Son, *by means of which it is united* to the humanity.'[4]

De Lugo continues: 'The Personality is not (*forma deificans*) that which deifies, nevertheless the Deity formally deifies the humanity by means of the Personality (*mediante personalitate*), not that this is the cause of deification, but because it is the *condition necessary to this effect*, namely, that the Deity may deify (the humanity).'[5]

The humanity subsisting in the hypostatic union is therefore deified mediately, that is by union with the Divine Nature.

He argues farther: 'We cannot conceive the Humanity of Christ as united to the Word, or, as having union with the Word, without (*eo ipso*) by that conception itself predicating that the Humanity is denominated and *deified* by the Word : *for what else is union with the Word, but being informed, as I may say, or deified by the Word.*'[6]

---

[4] *De Incarn.* dis. xvi. sect. ii. 39.   [5] Ib. 48.

[6] Ib. s. 48. So also in s. 49.

APPENDIX II.

THE ADORATION OF THE DEIFIED HUMANITY.

THE passages given already in the note to pages 23-4 are enough to show that the Catholic Church in adoring the Incarnate Word with the divine worship of latria has from the beginning consciously and distinctly regarded the Deified Humanity as partaking in that one Divine Adoration.

The three following passages of Holy Scripture are used commonly by the Fathers as proof:

1. 'When He bringeth in the First-begotten into the world He saith : And let all the angels of God adore Him'—that is, the Incarnate Son.[7]

2. 'For which cause God also hath exalted Him, and hath given Him a name which is above all names : that at the name of Jesus every knee shall bow, of those that are in heaven, on earth, and under the earth : and that every tongue shall confess that the Lord Jesus Christ is in the glory of God the Father'—that is, Jesus, God and Man.[8]

3. 'Adore the footstool of His feet, for it is holy.'[9]

S. Ambrose interprets this as follows: 'By the word footstool the earth is to be understood, and by

[7] Heb. i. 6.   [8] Phil. ii. 9-11.   [9] Ps. xcviii. 5.

the earth the Flesh of Christ, which to-day also we adore in a mystery, and which the Apostles worshipped in the Lord Jesus, as we before said. For Christ is not divided, but is one.'[10]

S. Augustine also says: 'He took earth from the earth, because flesh is of earth, and He received flesh from the flesh of Mary. . . . No one eats that flesh except he has first adored it; and thus we have shown how such a footstool of the Lord's feet is adored; and not only do we not sin in adoring it, but we sin in not adoring it.'[11]

S. Athanasius is still more explicit: 'We do not adore a creature; God forbid. Such madness belongs to heathens and to Arians. But we adore the Lord of things created, the Incarnate Word of God. For though the flesh itself by itself be a part of things created, yet it is made the body of God. Neither do we adore His body divided and apart from the Word; nor when we adore the Word do we separate the Word from the flesh: for inasmuch as we know that the Word was made flesh, we acknowledge God the Word dwelling in the flesh.'[12]

S. John Damascene: 'Christ therefore is one,

10 *De Spiritu Sancto.* lib. iii. 79.
11 *Enarr. in Ps.* xcviii. 9.
12 *Epist. ad Adelph.* sect. 3.

perfect God and perfect Man, whom we adore with the Father and the Holy Ghost in one adoration, with His immaculate flesh.'[13]

S. Ildephonsus of Toledo: 'As to which mystery Cyril, answering Nestorius, declares Christ to be so one, that is God and Man: not as if we adore a man with the Word, lest by this a certain division be introduced; but adoring one and the same (object) in the unity of the Person: for the body (of the Word) is not apart from the Word, nor diverse, because the Word was made flesh: and manhood is so united and assumed into God as to be one God.'[14]

Thomassinus sums up the patristic doctrine in this proposition: 'That the Word made Flesh is worshipped with the one adoration of latria: and that thus the Humanity also is enveloped in the worship of latria.'[15]

Nestorius was required under anathema by the Synod of Alexandria under S. Cyril to subscribe to the following canon: 'If any one shall dare to say that the man assumed is to be adored *together* with God the Word and to be glorified *together* with Him, *as one thing with another* (*i.e.* as two things), and

---

[13] *De Fide Orthodoxa*, lib. iii. cap. 8.
[14] *Fragm. de partu Virginis*, tom. ix. Bibl. Patr.
[15] *De Incarn. Verb.* lib. xi. c. 2.

not that Emmanuel should rather be adored *with one adoration :* let him be anathema.'[16]

So also a Lateran Council under Martin I. repeats the doctrine of the Fourth and Fifth Œcumenical Councils. It quotes the ninth canon of the Fifth Œcumenical Council as follows : 'If any man shall say that Christ is to be adored in two natures, *by which they bring in two adorations*, to God the Word *separately* and to the man *separately ;* or if any man so adore Christ, affirming the nature or essence of the two that are united to be one, so as to destroy the flesh or to confound the Godhead and the Manhood : and shall not adore with *one adoration* God the Word Incarnate with His flesh according to the tradition of the Church of God from the beginning : let him be anathema.'[17]

Petavius comments on this as follows : ' Hence it is evident from the consent and tradition of the Church as a fixed and established truth that the flesh or the nature of man with the Word is to be worshipped with one only, and that the divine and supreme adoration.'[18]

Tourneley says : ' The Human Nature of Christ

---

[16] Labbe, *Concilia*, tom. iii. p. 966, Conc. Ephcs.
[17] Ibid. tom. vii. p. 258, Conc. Lateran.
[18] *De Incarnatione*, lib. xv. cap. iii. par. 6.

hypostatically joined to the Word is to be worshipped with one and the same adoration as the Divine Word. . . . Hence we may easily solve the following common and trite objection : viz. the worship of latria is due to God alone.   The Humanity of Christ is not God : therefore the worship of latria is not due to it.   Here we must distinguish the minor proposition : the Humanity is not God, separated and apart from the Word, granted ; but hypostatically united with the Word, I deny it'—*i.c.* it is God.[19]

Perrone : ' The Human Nature of Christ is to be adored with one and the same worship of latria in the Divine Word, with whom it is hypostatically united.   This proposition is *de fide*, and its contradictory was condemned in the Fifth General Council.'[20]

Franzelin : ' Christ is to be adored, both regarded as to His Divine Nature and regarded as to His Human Nature, with one and the same supreme worship of latria.'[21]

The Würzburg Theology : ' *Question :* Is Christ to be worshipped with religious worship, not only as God, which is self-evident, but also as Man ? *An-*

---

[19] *De Incarnatione*, tom. iv. quæst. ult. p. 425.
[20] Ibid. p. ii. c. iv. art. 2, prop. i.
[21] *De Verb. Incarn.* cap. iv. th. xlv.

swer : Christ as Man, subsisting in both divine and human nature, that is the Man-God; or the human nature of Christ hypostatically united to the Word, is to be worshipped absolutely with one and the same act of latria as the Divine Word.'[22]

APPENDIX III.

THE ADORATION OF THE SACRED HEART.

The Sacred Humanity hypostatically united to the Word, and all parts thereof, espècially the Sacred Heart of Jesus, are the object of divine adoration.[23]

I. Christ God and Man is to be adored with one and the same divine adoration in both natures. The material object (*objectum materiale*) of this divine adoration is Christ, God and Man; the formal object (*objectum formale*), by reason of which this divine adoration is given to Him in both natures, is the Godhead of the Incarnate Son.

II. The Sacred Humanity, or Human Nature, inasmuch as it is the human nature of the Word, is the partial object (*objectum partiale*) which is adored

----

[22] *De Incarnatione*, dis. v. sect. lii. art. 1.
[23] Franzelin, *De Verbo Incarn.* cap. vi. th. xlv. p. 453.

with divine worship; for as the Person of Christ, including His human nature, is the object of divine adoration, the worship which is due to His Person is due to all that is united to His Person : for this cause the Fifth General Œcumenical Council condemned the Nestorians, who introduced two adorations as to two separate natures and to two separate persons. It condemned also those who, as the Apollinaristæ and Eutychians, affirmed the adoration to be one, because one nature alone was to be adored ; viz. the Divine, excluding the humanity. The Council affirms that one adoration is to be offered to the Word together with His flesh, so that the flesh also is the object, because it is the flesh of the Word who is adored as one whole object.

III. The calumnies of the ancient Nestorians and Monophysites were renewed by the Jansenists, who affirmed, with the Apollinaristæ, that the human nature could not be adored because it was a creature, and therefore denounced the Catholics as *sarkolatræ* and *anthropolatræ* (*i.e.* worshippers of the flesh and worshippers of man).

IV. The Incarnation is the manifestation of God. S. John says expressly, ' The Word was made flesh, and dwelt among us, and we saw His glory ;'[24] and,

___

[24] S. John i. 14.

again, 'That which was from the beginning, which we have heard, which we have seen with our eyes, which we have looked upon and our hands have handled of the word of life; for the life was manifested, and we have seen and do bear witness.'[25] The Incarnate Word, therefore, manifests Himself to us to be adored in His human nature. We may adore Him in all His divine perfections, in His infinite goodness, love, mercy, wisdom, omnipotence, manifested in His Incarnation. We may adore Him also as He manifests Himself to us in all the actions and sufferings of His Incarnate Person, in His Nativity, His Infancy, His Passion, His Death, His Resurrection, His glory at the right hand of the Father. S. Thomas adored Him in the manifestation of His Five Sacred Wounds; we adore Him also in His Sacred Heart.

V. Of this devotion Franzelin says, that it was 'assailed by the Jansenists with incoherent clamours and calumnies not less absurd than impudent.'[26] He adds, that certain Catholics in the time of the Synod of Pistoia joined in the cry. His answer to them is as follows: It never came into the mind of anybody but of certain absurd accusers that the Sacred Heart of Jesus is to be worshipped

<hr>

[25] S. John i. 2.   [26] *De Verbo Incarnato*, p. 465.

and adored either divided from the humanity or separate from the hypostatic union or the Divine Person whose humanity it is. This false and wanton accusation was condemned in the Bull *Auctorem Fidei*, by which also the Synod of Pistoia was condemned in the following words : ' The proposition which asserts "*to adore the humanity of Christ directly, much more any part of it, would always be to give divine honours to a creature*," inasmuch as by this word *directly* it is intended to reprobate the divine adoration which the faithful give to the humanity of Christ, as if such adoration by which the humanity and the life-giving flesh of Christ is adored, not indeed for its own sake and as if mere flesh (*non quidem propter se et tanquam nuda caro*), but as it is united to the Divinity, would be divine honour given to a creature, and not that one and the same adoration by which the Word Incarnate with His own flesh is adored according to the Fifth General Council of Constantinople, canon ix., is a proposition false, captious, derogatory, and injurious to the pious and due adoration given and to be given by the faithful to the humanity of Christ.[27]

' The doctrine which rejects the devotion of the Sacred Heart of Jesus as among devotions described

---

[27] Const. Pii VI., Auctorem Fidei, prop. 61.

as new, erroneous, or at least dangerous, if understood of this devotion such as the Holy See has approved, is false, rash, pernicious, offensive to pious ears, and injurious to the Holy See.[28]

'Also, inasmuch as it censures the worshippers of the Heart of Jesus even by that name *for not perceiving that the sacred flesh of Christ, or any part of the same, or even the whole humanity when separated and divided from the divinity, cannot be adored with the worship of latria*—as if the faithful do adore the Heart of Jesus *separated* or *divided* from the Divinity, while they adore it as it is the Heart of Jesus, the Heart, that is, of the Person of the Word. to whom it is *inseparably united* in the same way as the bloodless Body of Christ in the three days of death was adorable in the sepulchre without separation or division from the Divinity—(is a proposition) captious and injurious to the faithful who worship the Heart of Christ.'[29]

After quoting certain extravagant absurdities of this kind, published by Camillus Blasius in 1771, Franzelin justly adds: 'The pestilence which is called party-spirit at times renders even acute men *furiose stupidos.*'[30]

VI. Among other objections to the worship of

<hr>

[28] Prop. 62.   [29] Ib. 63.   [30] *De Verb. Incarn.* p. 467 note.

the Sacred Heart is one which comes from those whose common sense and Christian faith preserved them from the absurdity of feigning a heart separate or divided from the Incarnate Word. They admit that divine worship is due to the Sacred Humanity in the Person of the Incarnate Word, and to the Sacred Heart in that Sacred Humanity; but they affirm that the object of this devotion is the Sacred Heart, not in itself, but as a mere symbol of the love of Jesus. If then the Heart of Jesus is worshipped as a symbol of the love of Jesus, how can it be that the object of this worship is not real? The Heart of Jesus cannot be worshipped as a symbol of charity without worshipping the Heart of Jesus itself. But this question is doubly set at rest, first by Pius the Sixth in the Bull *Auctorem Fidei* above quoted, in which the Pontiff declares that the faithful adore the Heart of Jesus as it is the Heart of Jesus, the Heart, that is, of the Person of the Word, to whom it is inseparably united, in the same way as the bloodless Body of Christ in the three days of death was adored in the sepulchre without separation or division from the Divinity. And, once more, Pius the Ninth, in the Apostolic Letters of Beatification of Blessed Margaret Mary, August 19, 1864, says : ' Jesus, the Author and Finisher of our Faith, desired nothing

more than to kindle the flame of charity by which
His Heart was burning in all ways in the hearts of
men; . . . . but that He might the more kindle this
fire of charity, it was His will that the veneration
and worship of His Sacred Heart should be instituted
and promoted: . . . to Blessed Margaret, fervently
praying before the Most August Sacrament of the
Eucharist it was made known by Christ our Lord,
that it would be most grateful to Him if the worship
of His Most Sacred Heart, burning with the fire of
charity for mankind, should be instituted.'

The Sacred Heart, therefore, which we adore is
the human Heart that the Son of God took from
the substance of His Immaculate Mother, and in
taking deified it.   It is the Heart of God, living and
life-giving, adored with divine worship in heaven and
earth, at the right hand of His Father, and in His
real presence in the Most Holy Sacrament of the
Altar.

II.

THE SACRED HEART GOD'S WAY OF LOVE.

THE SACRED HEART GOD'S WAY OF LOVE.

No man hath seen God at any time: the only-begotten Son, who is in the bosom of the Father, He hath declared Him. S. JOHN i. 18.

'No man hath seen God at any time.' Therefore the fool said in his heart, 'There is no God;' for that which cannot be seen, to the fool does not exist. But if there be a truth certain to the reason, it is the existence of God. I am certain of my own existence because I am conscious of it. I need not reason about it; I make no syllogism; my existence is not a conclusion from premises. I know the existence of the natural world because my senses assure me of it, and I need no further evidence. My intellect tells me of the existence of God because it is a necessity of my reason to believe that, as the Apostle writes, 'Every house is built by some man. He that created all things is God.'[1] And I could as soon believe that this cathedral in which

[1] Heb. iii. 4.

we are gathered together was reared by fortuitous action, or piled itself up by a spontaneous volition of its own, as that the world that we see had no Maker; and I am confirmed in this necessity of my reason by the fact that the whole race of mankind has believed in the existence of God. Men may have multiplied their gods; but that proves all the more. They may have distorted their conceptions of God, they may have depraved them, they may have weakened them almost to the verge of extinction; but there is not to be found a nation or a race in the whole family of mankind that has not had an idea of God to deprave; that is, a tradition of His existence. I say this, not to prove the existence of God by counting the number of votes, either of nations or of men; but I adduce it to prove the existence of a necessity of the reason, of a rational law by which an intelligent being is coerced by the very action of his intelligence to believe in the existence of God. Moreover, I find in myself, and I trace in the whole history of man, a consciousness of the distinction of right from wrong—a belief that there is a law of right, and that to transgress it is wrong; and as there is the notion of the law, so there is the notion of the lawgiver. And therefore I say once more that if there be anything certain to the reason, it is that God exists, and that God is the Maker of all things and the Judge of all men. That being so, I affirm that it is most fitting that God should become incarnate; that there is no incongruity, nothing incoherent, nothing unworthy of the Divine Nature, in the Incarnation of God.

It is my purpose to speak upon four points. The first will be what I have just said: the fitness of the Incarnation; that is to say, that it is most consistent with the wisdom and the glory of God that His Son should become incarnate. Secondly, I purpose to show that what is called dogma is at the same time devotion; and that they who imagine that dogma is indevotional or hinders devotion simply show that they do not comprehend what dogma is, and, I may say, what is truth itself. Thirdly, we shall have to speak of the five ways of knowing the Sacred Heart. And lastly, we shall speak of the presence of Jesus in the Most Holy Sacrament of the Altar, and of the character of His Sacred Heart therein to us.

Now inasmuch as some have said that for God to be made man has unfitness in itself, I affirm that the Incarnation is in a high degree fitting, and in harmony with the Divine Nature, and therefore most convenient, that is to say, in strict agreement with the nature of God and of man. And further, I purpose to show that it is most for the glory of God, and that if God had not been incarnate one great manifestation of His glory would not have been given ; that in the Incarnation God has both glorified Himself and deified our humanity, and that He has made us partakers of His glory and of a Divine Nature by making us members of Christ ; and that therefore to that essential glory which He had from all eternity — namely, the mutual knowledge and love of the Ever-blessed Trinity—He has added the highest accidental glory, in the greatest possible knowledge and love and adoration on the part of His creatures. This, then in outline is that of which I wish to speak.

1. And first I will begin by affirming this evident truth, that by the Incarnation God has placed Himself within the range of the human intelligence, and thereby has enabled man to know Him with a fulness and a precision which was not possible be—fore. What was the range of the knowledge of the first man in Paradise it is not easy for us to say. That he had a knowledge by supernatural light, that he knew God, and that by the light of faith he saw God—not as a whole (that is impossible, for God is infinite), but in His perfections—is certain. As

we who see the firmament see the whole heavens, though they extend beyond our sight—for we see the heavenly bodies, and in seeing them we form a conception of all that we cannot see—so Adam, by supernatural light and by the supernatural intelligence which came with it, knew God.   But this was clouded by his sin ; and we, in the state in which we are, even with the light of faith, are darkened by his fall.   Our weakened intelligence limits our knowledge of God.   The conception of God in His infinitude and His eternity and His boundless perfections transcends our faculties and overwhelms our intelligence.   And therefore, in order to make the knowledge of Himself easier and more intimate to us, God became incarnate.   He came into the midst of mankind in the dimensions of our manhood.   He enabled us to comprehend His infinite presence by a presence which is finite.   He was verily and truly and personally present by the manhood which He assumed ; and that manhood was of the same dimensions and stature as ours.   They who looked upon the face of Jesus Christ saw God.   And further, in manifesting that finite presence of the Infinite God He also manifested the infinite perfections of God in the finite perfections of His deified manhood. The sanctity and the love and the truth and the mercy of Jesus were the very same divine attributes and perfections as the sanctity, mercy, justice, and truth of God. And further, there was a finite image of God visible to man which was the very and true manifestation of the infinite image of God. The only-begotten Son, who is in the bosom of the Father, is the Brightness of His Father's glory, the Figure of His substance, the express Image of the invisible God. These are three titles given to Him by the Holy Ghost. And the Infinite Image of God, the Eternal and Uncreated Intelligence of God—that is, the Son of God—took upon Himself our humanity, which was also created to God's image and likeness. The Infinite Image of God clothed in our humanity united both the original and the likeness in one Person; and thereby the conception of God became to man more intimate, more facile, more intelligible, more within the sphere of the human reason. And whereas before, the nations of the world who had lost the true knowledge of the invisible God had formed to themselves both mental and material idols—that is, local, finite, and human conceptions of God— God abolished them by taking our humanity upon Himself, manifesting Himself to sense and to reason by a finite presence; and by that presence of His deified humanity He destroyed, as by the flood of light which when the sun rises fills the world, all false images and false conceptions of the infinite God fashioned for itself by the darkened heart of man. The words therefore of the Apostle are strictly true in this: 'God, who commanded the light to shine out of darkness, hath shined in our hearts, to give the light of the knowledge of the glory of God, in the face of Jesus Christ.'[2]   The Sacred Countenance of the incarnate Son of God arose upon the world as the Sun of the New Creation, the Mirror of God; and all those who saw Him saw God.   Therefore He said: 'Do you not believe that I am in the Father, and the Father in Me? He that seeth Me seeth the Father also;'[3] for 'I and the Father are one.'[4]   And so it came to pass that God, who from the creation was present in all things in a divine manner—for He was present by His essence, which sustains the being of all created things; He was with them also by His sovereignty, which impresses a law upon all things, and by His power, which preserves all His works —to this threefold manner of presence added a fourth, that is, by Incarnation. The Creator came into the midst of His creatures as if He were one

<hr>

[2] 2 Cor. iv. 6.   [3] S. John xiv. 9, 10.   [4] Ib. x. 30.

of them. He took upon Himself our humanity; and He thereby became visible and palpable. As afterwards He met the unbelief of Thomas, so in the Incarnation He meets the folly of the fool, who, because 'no man hath seen God at any time,' said there is no God. He came and He showed Himself; so that man, by the report of his own senses to his own rational intelligence, should know, by a new and more explicit testimony, and that the testimony of reason, that there is a God.

2. Then, once more, by the Incarnation God placed Himself in like manner within the range of our hearts. There is nothing in the whole history of the world more fearful than the corruption of the heart of man under false conceptions of God. Heathenism is man without God, and for that reason corrupted. There is not a passion or a vice of human nature which was not deified by the pagan world. The very adorations which they paid to the monstrous gods of their own conception were, like their idols, horrible and not to be described. Therefore God, for the purification and sanctification of the human heart, placed Himself within the sphere of our affections: He has made it easy to know Him, and therefore easy to love Him. He revealed Himself of old to Prophets, to Patriarchs, and to His own people.

The personal nature of God was known and understood by the line of the faithful at all times, and especially by the family of Israel, to whom God gave a large and abundant revelation of Himself in His divine personality by His incomprehensible Name, 'I am who am.' The power, the love, the mercy of God—all these great moral attributes were revealed to them. But that He might make them more intimate with the heart of God, He took for Himself a nature like our own; He came as a man into the midst of men; He came to gaze upon men with a human countenance, to speak to men with a human voice, to love men with a human heart, that men might see, united in His Person, the Creator and the creature, the Infinite and the finite, the Divine and the human, that is, in the hypostatic union of manhood with God. In Him was revealed the fountain of all the gifts of grace: the fountain of life which in eternity was in the bosom of God, on the eternal Hills. The River of life came down through the Sacred Heart of Jesus, and from Him has spread to all nations. 'The Word was made flesh, and dwelt amongst us; and we saw His glory, the glory of the Only-begotten of the Father, full of grace and truth.' He revealed thereby the divine characteristics of love, pity, compassion, mercy, tenderness, long-suffering, and generosity. The Word made flesh bore upon Him the whole impress and delineation of God. The eternal character of God shone through the transparent perfections of His human character. It was the human interpretation of the divine nature. And what was the character so revealed? In one word, it was 'God is charity.' The essence of God is charity, and the essence of God is Himself. God is charity; and that Charity was incarnate, and that Charity came and was passible among men. He came to weep over the sins of men, to weep at the grave of the dead, to weep over the sins of Jerusalem, to suffer, to hunger, to thirst, to be in agony, and to be crucified. What, then, is our conception of the Divine Nature through the Incarnation? Love, sorrowing, suffering, and dying for us. It is not possible for the eternal perfections of the love of God to be more intelligible than God has made them by the Incarnation of His Son. 'No man hath seen God,' indeed, 'at any time; but the Only-begotten Son, who is in the bosom of the Father,' and Who was made man for us, to suffer and to sorrow and to die, 'hath declared Him.'

3. And then, once more, God was made man in order to create in the minds of men a consciousness, lost by sin, of the love of God to them. Throughout

the whole world, outside the people of Israel, every conception of God was terrible and full of fear. The worship of God was the propitiation of wayward, irresistible, and avenging powers. The thought of a God who is love, pity, compassion, purity, and holiness indeed, but full of mercy, was a conception not to be found except in revelation. The highest conception of God was imperfect until the Incarnation. Then it received its fulness, when God made man was manifest, and manifested in Himself the character of God. A consciousness was then awakened in the hearts of men that God loves man, and that there is no love, of which the human heart can form a conception, such as is the love of God for fervour, for tenderness, for generosity. There is no love that can be believed by the heart of man like the love of God. And because the love of an invisible, inscrutable, spiritual, and Eternal Being was hard for the heart of man to conceive, God therefore manifested Himself in our humanity, that is, He came to assure us of His love as a kinsman speaking to kinsmen. He took not upon Him the nature of angels, because He did not come to redeem angels; but He took upon Him the nature of man, because He came to redeem mankind. If He had taken upon Himself the nature of angels, He could not have suffered as man; and if He had come in the form of an angel He would not have been our kinsman, for we are not of the kindred of angels. 'He took upon Himself,' therefore, as the Apostle says, ' to be a partaker of flesh and blood, that through death He might destroy him who hath the empire of death.' He came in our humanity as our kinsman, and He spoke to us as a kinsman ; and we know, if in a foreign land we meet with one of our own race, one of our own people, how our hearts warm to him in the midst of strangers. A secret but sure attraction draws us to him as if he were more than friend. What, then, was the effect of the Incarnation when God came into the midst of men ; when He manifested Himself as the Kinsman of men; and when He came, not only as the Kinsman, but as the Brother, as one who had the same Father—one too who had the same Mother, for He took our humanity of her substance? He came too as one who had the same home, and could say, ' In My Father's house there are many mansions : I go to prepare a place for you.' And He came, not only as a brother, but as a friend,—for all kinsmen are not brothers, and all brothers are not friends. He came as a friend, as one who had the same will with us, in so far as our will is right—that is to say, so far as our will is towards that which is for our happiness and our salvation ; and He proved all this by dying for us.   He came as our Saviour, as our Redeemer from death and from sin, from which doom we could not save ourselves.   And why was all this? That by all these things He might draw our hearts upwards into the love of God: that from the love of kinsman to the love of brother, from the love of brother to the love of friend, from the love of friend to the love of Saviour, from the love of Saviour to the love of God, He might draw all hearts to Himself, and with them ascend into heaven; so that the words of the Apostle are true to the very letter, 'Therefore if you be risen with Christ seek the things that are above, where Christ is sitting at the right hand of God.   Mind the things that are above, not the things that are upon the earth.   For you are dead, and your life is hid with Christ in God.'[5]   He was raising up the heart of man little by little, that by the consciousness of the love of God He might make men to love God.   All this manifestation of personal love was a divine means of winning back again the hearts of men.   God has an infinite power of command; but even the power of command in God Himself cannot make man love Him.   The infinite power of the word of God is such that when He said, 'Let there be light,' there was light.   At His word all

<hr>

[5] Col. iii. 1-3.

creation sprang into existence; the command of God went forth, and it was done. But the command of God from the beginning has been saying, 'Thou shalt love the Lord thy God with thy whole heart;' and we have not obeyed. Man will not do what God commands; and no commandment can bend or win the will of man. And why? Because the heart of man is cold, because the heart of man is hard with love of self, and because in the heart of man there is a free will which is averted from God. All the commandments of God are not enough to make us love Him, and that because nothing but a flame will kindle flame; a stream of water will not kindle fire, but a spark will kindle a conflagration, because it is of the same nature. A loving heart alone therefore can kindle love, and Love was incarnate in order to kindle love in man. The Charity of God was made man, that our hearts might be made to burn with the love of God. Our Lord has declared it: 'I am come to send fire upon the earth; and what do I desire but that it should be kindled?' He knew that, as love alone can kindle love, love alone can feed and sustain love. If we kindle a fire, unless we tend and feed it, soon or late it will die out. So is it with the love of God. If God should kindle the love of Himself in our hearts, He must keep it alive. Unless He sustain and feed it by a perpetual reviving of the motives of love, our selfishness would soon leave off to love Him. And this He has done for ever through the Sacred Heart of His Incarnate Son. As love alone can kindle love and alone can feed and sustain it, so love alone can make love perfect. Nothing but the Divine Love made Man, and thereby united with us, and, more than this, dwelling in us, can bring our love to perfection. But 'God is charity; and he that abideth in charity abideth in God, and God in him;'[6] and in every Communion of the Precious Body and Blood of Jesus Christ you receive the Sacred Heart, that is, you receive the Incarnate Love of God into your heart.

4. And further: God has provided in the Incarnation a fourth way of presence in the world. He thereby has opened a way by which the consciousness of His presence may be perpetually sustained in all those who have hearts to believe. Why is it that men who call themselves Christians wander to and fro, so cold, so careless, and so forgetful of God? It is because they have not a recollection, nor even a consciousness of His presence. If they lived and moved in the presence of God as they do in the light of the noonday sun, if they were as

[6] 1 S. John iv. 16.

conscious of their relation to God and God's relation to them as they are of the relations they bear
to those that are about them in life, then their
whole being and their work here would be governed
by that sense. But it is not so with us. Therefore that He might bring this home with all the
intimate force of a constant remembrance, He constituted Himself to be the Head of the Body of
which we are members. In so far as we are united
to Him, the Head of that Body is present in us. He
is in the whole Church, and in every member of
it. In the measure in which we are united to
Him, in that measure the consciousness and the
recollection of His presence will be continually
sustained in us. If at any time it be not so, the
fault is ours. But that same consciousness of His
presence as God and Man, and as Head of the
Church in all its members, is always and everywhere sustained by the perpetual presence of the
Most Holy Eucharist. The visible Church upon
earth is, I may say, the Tabernacle in which abides
the Incarnate Word present upon every altar. The
Church is one wide sanctuary, it is the guest-
chamber spread in all the world, in which Jesus
gave this last commandment of His love. The
visible Church in the world hangs as a canopy over

that Sacred Presence; and every altar in the Catholic unity is but one altar, as the Most Holy Sacrament upon every altar is but one Sacrament, one mystery of the 'Word made flesh,' dwelling for ever in the midst of us. The consciousness of His presence is made thereby intimate and perpetual and universal. Therefore, in all our daily life it ought to be with us. When you arise in the morning, you rise up disciples of Jesus Christ. Let it be the first thing you do, to kneel down at His feet. Go out to your daily life from His very side. As the Apostles, when they left their Master to do His bidding in Judea and in Galilee, so do you likewise. Day by day you leave the presence of Jesus Christ to go into your path in life, whatever it may be, and in that path of life He is with you everywhere. He is with you in the throng of men, in the solitude of your home, in your silent work, and in the midst of your busiest hours. If you are unconscious of His presence, He is there none the less. If you forget Him, you deprive yourselves of the strength and peace of knowing that you are never alone, and that He is ever with you.

Here, then, I have given sufficient reason to justify what I said: that the Incarnation has spread the knowledge of God into the sphere of our intelli-

gence and into the range of our affections; that it
has created in us a consciousness of the love of God
to us; that it has awakened the love of man to God;
and that it has created and perpetuated a sense
of His presence with us in a way ineffable, because
divine.   It is indeed a love exceeding all that our
heart can conceive; it is the greatest exercise of
the omnipotence of God in the revelation of Himself.
If that be so, then the conclusion from what I have
said is this: that the Sacred Heart is a volume of
light, in which the knowledge and the love of God
are written within and without.   When Jesus said,
'I am the Way, the Truth, and the Life,' He
meant to say, 'Everything is contained in Me;'
'No man cometh unto the Father but by Me;'[7] there
is no other path or gate.   In Him 'are hid all
the treasures of wisdom and knowledge;'[8] that
is to say, no man can know God truly except by
Jesus Christ; no man can truly know the True God
except by the light of faith; no man can have the
light of faith except by the grace of the Holy Ghost,
Who comes to us through Jesus Christ: and by
that light of faith we come to the Father, through
the merits of the Incarnate Son.   There is no other
way to life.   No man can come to God by any

[7] S. John xiv. 6.   [8] Col. ii. 3.

merits of his own, but solely and only through the merits of the Incarnate Son. No man can come to the Father except by the light of the teaching of Jesus Christ, and no man can come to Jesus Christ except the Father, who hath sent Him, shall draw him.[9] Therefore, He is the Way, and the only way to the Father. And when He said, 'I am the gate; by Me, if any man shall enter in, he shall be saved, and he shall go in and go out and find pasture,'[10] He meant precisely this: it is only through His merits, through His teaching, through His grace, and therefore through His Sacred Heart, that we can come to the Father. But He said not only 'I am the Way,' He said also 'I am the Truth.' All the truth of God is summed up in the Incarnation. We shall see this more fully hereafter. It is enough at this time to say that 'in Jesus,' as the Apostle said, 'dwelt all the fulness of the Godhead corporally;'[11] that is, the Sacred Heart of Jesus is the most glorious throne of God; for where the Son is, there is the Father and the Holy Ghost—the Son Incarnate, the Father not Incarnate, nor the Holy Ghost Incarnate, but all three consubstantial in one Godhead. But being consubstantial, wheresoever is the Person of the Son, there is the Person of the

[9] S. John vi. 44.   [10] Ib. x. 9.   [11] Col. ii. 9.

Father and there the Person of the Holy Ghost. And the Sacred Heart is therefore the throne of the Ever-blessed Trinity. It is the most glorious Kingdom of God the Father, in which He reigns over that Divine Heart—human like ours—with the most perfect sway of His Wisdom and His Love, receiving from it in return the most perfect obedience of which a human heart is capable. And so also the Sacred Heart is the holiest and the highest sanctuary of the Son. The sanctuary where He dwells in the Blessed Sacrament is the type of that sanctuary of the Sacred Heart in which He personally dwells by incarnation. And the Heart of Jesus is also the mightiest instrument of the Holy Ghost, whereby He draws souls to salvation, whereby He reveals the mysteries of the Ever-blessed Trinity, whereby He accomplishes the works of grace in the world. And as He is 'the Way' and 'the Truth,' so He is 'the Life'—eternal life even now to those in whom He dwells.

And, lastly, to sum all up in a word. As the Incarnation is God's Book of Life, the knowledge of His Sacred Heart is the interpretation and the unfolding of that Book. The whole mystery of God and of man, and the relations of God and man in grace and in glory, are all written in the Sacred

Heart. They that know the Sacred Heart know God; they that love the Sacred Heart love God; and they that are made like to the Sacred Heart are made like to God. It is the compendium of the whole science of God, of the whole way of salvation, of the whole gospel of eternal life.

And, therefore, to repeat what I said in the beginning, the Incarnation has a fitness and a convenience in the ways of God to man, and an adaptation to the nature and to the needs of man; to his intelligence, to his heart, and to his will. God had already, I may say, spoken by His presence through His whole inanimate creation; for God is manifested by all His works. His power and His divinity are known 'by the things which are made.' But this was not enough to make Himself palpable to sense, intelligible as an object of the intellect, and intimate as an object of love to the heart. What yet remained possible? If He had assumed the nature of angels, it would not have been enough; there would still have been a gulf between Him and us. He therefore assumed our humanity. He could come no nearer. He could not make Himself more intelligible than by a human voice and a human form. He could not make Himself the object of human love more intimatley than by loving us with a human heart. Therefore, instead of incongruity—as the wise men of this world, who will not believe, so proudly and so wildly say—the Incarnation is the most luminous revelation of the perfect wisdom of God. He who knows what is in man, and who knows His own perfection, glorified Himself above measure in that His Son was incarnate for our sakes. This, then, is the declaration we have received from Him : 'God is light'—that is, Truth and Purity—' and in Him there is no darkness. If we say we have fellowship with Him and walk in darkness'—that is, commit sin—'we lie, and do not the truth ; but if we walk in the light'—that is, in purity and truth— ' as He is in the light, then we have fellowship one with another, and the Blood of Jesus Christ His Son cleanseth us from all sin.'[12]

[12] 1 S. John i. 5-7.

III.

DOGMA THE SOURCE OF DEVOTION.

DOGMA THE SOURCE OF DEVOTION.

You adore that which you know not. We adore that which we know. S. John iv. 22.

Jesus is the Book of Life, and in Him 'are hid all the treasures of wisdom and knowledge,' of Him alone all the mysteries of the Kingdom of God may be learnt; not only because He is the Divine Teacher, but because they are all contained in the knowledge of Himself. When He said, 'I am the Way, the Truth, and the Life; no man cometh unto the Father but by Me,' He declared that all truth was contained in Himself; and when the Apostle said that he judged himself to 'know nothing save Jesus Christ and Him crucified,'[1] he meant the same thing, namely, that he who knows Jesus Christ aright knows the whole Revelation of God. As the radiance which flows from the sun is inseparable from the sun, so is the Revelation of God the radiance which flows from the Person of Jesus Christ. I have said

[1] 1 Cor. ii. 2.

that the Sacred Heart is the key or interpretation of the Incarnation of the Eternal Word. Any one who desires to know the mystery of the Incarnation—and in that mystery of the Incarnation to know, I will say, the whole Science of God—may learn it by reading the Sacred Heart of our Divine Redeemer. And they who know that Science of God know also what I may call the science of man—that is, of our human nature—in Him and in ourselves; and they know likewise the relations between God and man and between us men, each to the other. And in these things are summed up the whole revelation of God. They who know these three things fully will know all that God has revealed for our salvation.

Now our Divine Lord, speaking to the woman of Samaria, said, 'You adore that which you know not;' because they were an idolatrous people, of mixed race, partly of Israel, partly of the nations brought and planted in a portion of the Promised Land. They had intermarried with the people of Israel, they had received the books of the Pentateuch, and they had a sort of fragmentary knowledge of the old revelation; but they did not rightly know the True God; and so much as they did know of the True God, they did not know truly. Therefore they could not worship Him 'in spirit and in truth.' For this cause our Divine Lord said, 'You worship that which you know not;' and He then further said, 'We adore that which we know, for salvation is of the Jews.' The full and pure light of revelation is in Jerusalem. The true knowledge of the True God is with us; and yet the time is coming when 'they that adore shall adore neither in this mountain nor in Jerusalem, but everywhere in spirit and in truth.'

From these words I draw one conclusion, namely, that knowledge is the first and vital condition of all true worship. You will remember how S. Paul at Athens found an altar 'to the unknown God,' and how he commended the people for their intentions of piety, but reproved them for their ignorance. He said, 'Him whom you ignorantly worship, Him I declare unto you.' Without knowledge there can be no adoration 'in spirit and in truth;' and just in the measure of our knowledge will our adoration be more or less perfect, that is, intelligent and spiritual. If our knowledge be full and perfect, so will our adoration be. From this let us draw two consequences, and then pass on.

The first is this. How great is the superstition of those who for centuries have pleased themselves by accusing the Catholic Church of teaching that 'ignorance is the mother of devotion.' The othe-

consequence is: that the mother of all true knowledge relating to God, and therefore the mother of all true worship, is the Holy Catholic Church alone. Is it not a masterpiece of craft that the father of lies should have so darkened the under-standings of our adversaries as to lead them into the profound superstition of believing that we keep people in ignorance in order to make them devout? My purpose, then, will be to trace out the connection between what the world scornfully calls dogma and devotion, or the worship of God 'in spirit and in truth.'

1. Now, first of all, let us see what is dogma. In the mouth of the world it means some positive, imperious, and overbearing assertion of a human authority, or of a self-confident mind. But what does it mean in the mouth of the Church? It means the precise enunciation of a divine truth, of a divine fact, or of a divine reality fully known, so far as it is the will of God to reveal it, adequately defined in words chosen and sanctioned by a divine authority.

It is the precise enunciation of a divine truth or of a divine reality; for instance, the nature and the personality of God, the Incarnation, the coming of the Holy Ghost, and suchlike truths and realities of the mind of God, precisely known, intellectually conceived, as God has revealed or accomplished them.   Every divine truth or reality, so far as God has been pleased to reveal it to us, casts its perfect outline and image upon the human intelligence. His own mind, in which dwells all truth in all fulness and in all perfection, so far as He has revealed of His truth, is cast upon the surface of our mind, in the same way as the sun casts its own image upon the surface of the water, and the disc of the sun is perfectly reflected from its surface. So, in the intelligence of the Apostles, when, by the illumination of the Holy Ghost. on the Day of Pentecost, the revelation of God was cast upon the surface of their intellect, every divine truth had its perfect outline and image, not confused, nor in a fragmentary shape, but with a perfect and complete impression. For instance, that God is One in nature; that in God there are Three Persons, and one only Person in Jesus Christ.   Next, it is not enough that a truth should be definitely conceived; for if a teacher know the truth, and is not able to communicate it with accuracy, the learner will be but little the wiser.   And therefore God, who gave His truth, has given also a perpetual assistance, whereby the Apostles first, and His Church from that day to this, precisely and without erring declare to mankind the truth which

was revealed in the beginning; and in declaring
that truth the Church clothes it in words, in what
we call a terminology: and in the choice of those
terms the Church is also guided. There is an assistance, by which the Church does not err in selecting
the very language in which to express divine truth.
For who does not see that, if the Church were to err
in the selection of the words, the declaration of
truth must be obscured? We are conscious every
day that we know with perfect certainty what we
desire to say, but, from the difficulty of finding or
choosing our words, we cannot convey our meaning
to another. The Church is not a stammerer as we
are. The Church of God has a divine assistance
perpetually guiding it, to clothe in language, that is,
in adequate expression, the divine truth which God
has committed to her trust. Therefore a dogma
signifies a correct verbal expression of the truth cor-
rectly conceived and known. But, lastly, it is not
sufficient that it be clearly understood in the intellect and accurately expressed in words, unless the authority by which it is declared shall be divine; because
without a divine authority we cannot have a divine
certainty; without a divine authority we can have no
such assurance that the doctrine which we hear may
not be erroneous. The Apostles were such a divine

authority, for they spoke in the Name of their Master. Their successor to this day is the Church, which, taken as a whole, has been, by the assistance of the Holy Ghost, promised by our Divine Lord and never absent from it, perpetually sustained in the path of truth, and preserved from all error in the declaration of that truth. Therefore 'He that heareth you heareth Me' is true to this day. He that hears the voice of the Church hears the voice of its Divine Head, and its authority is therefore divine. This, then, is a dogma: a divine truth clearly understood in the intellect, precisely expressed in words and by a divine authority. There are many things which follow from this. First, it proves that the Church of God must be dogmatic: and that any body which is not dogmatic is not the Church of God. Any body or communion that disclaims a divine, and therefore infallible, authority cannot be dogmatic, because it is conscious that it may err. And therefore the Catholic Church alone, the Church which is one and undivided throughout the world, united with its centre in the Holy See,—this, and this alone, is a dogmatic Church (as the world reproachfully reminds us), and on that I build my proof that it alone is the Church of God. A teaching authority which is dogmatic and not infallible is a tyranny and a

nuisance : a tyranny, because it binds the consciences
of men by human authority, liable to err; and a
nuisance, because as it may err, in the long-run it
certainly will, and 'if the blind lead the blind, shall
they not both fall into the ditch ?' We see, then,
what dogma means. The Holy Catholic Church
always has been and always must be dogmatic. In
this, and in no other sense, is it dogmatic; for it
delivers nothing to us to be believed except upon
divine authority, and that which it so delivers was
revealed by God.

2. Let us next go on to see what is devotion.
Devotion, or worship, or adoration is the love and
veneration with which we regard God and His Divine
Truth. There can be no Divine Truth which ought
not to be an object of love and of veneration. Every
truth that God has revealed is the word of God; it
is the mind of Jesus Christ—it comes to us from a
divine voice. How is it possible that we can do
otherwise than love and venerate every such divine
declaration ? If, when a divine truth is declared to
us, our hearts do not turn to it, as the eye turns
to the light; if there be not in us an instinctive
yearning, which makes us promptly turn to the sound
of the divine voice, the fault is in our hearts; for
just in proportion as we know the truth we shall

be drawn towards it. Devotion, therefore, signifies the worship and love which by faith we offer first to God, to the Ever-blessed Trinity, and to the Three Persons one by one. When the Persons are known to us, our relations to those Persons become likewise known, and every relation carries with it duties and prompts us to affections. We shall see hereafter the application of these truths. For the present it is enough to say that, in the measure in which we know the truth, in that measure we shall have the motives of loving and of venerating it.

We may therefore understand the relation between dogma and devotion to be simply in this, that without knowledge we cannot have either a love or a veneration for truth. Our Lord said, 'You adore that which you know not;' and because they knew it not they could not 'adore in spirit and in truth.' S. Paul found some of the disciples who did not so much as know whether there were any Holy Ghost.[2] Could they have had any love and veneration for the Third Person of the Blessed Trinity, of whose coming, nay, of whose existence, they never heard? We may, indeed, love a person whom we have never seen; because S. Peter says of our Divine Lord, 'Whom not having seen you love;'[3] but we

<hr>

[2] Acts xix. 2.   [3] 1 S. Peter i. 8.

cannot love anybody of whom we do not know. We may know by hearsay and we may know by faith, and we may love those whom we know by faith and by hearsay; but we cannot love those of whom we never heard. Therefore it is a law of our nature that we can will nothing and can love nothing unless we first know it. The intellect is said in philosophy to carry a light before the will. What is called dogma, or divine truth, must go before all devotion; and in the proportion in which we have the light to know the objects of faith, in that proportion, if we be faithful, devotion will spring up in our hearts. Take this for an example. Our Divine Lord was in the midst of His disciples before He suffered; they knew Him to be 'a Teacher sent from God,' and they venerated and loved Him according to the knowledge which they had of Him and of the perfections of His Person. Peter, by an infused light from God, knew Him to be the 'Christ, the Son of the Living God;' but as yet they none of them knew Him in the fulness of His Godhead. After His Resurrection they began to know Him as God and as the Redeemer of the world; after His Ascension and the Day of Pentecost they knew Him as the King Eternal, and as their Saviour and Lord, who had redeemed them in His Precious Blood. In the measure in which their knowledge grew, grew also their love and their worship. So that, as a rule, we may say, wherever there is perfect knowledge there will be perfect worship; and wherever the knowledge varies more or less, in that proportion will vary love and veneration. Perfect worship, therefore, is only in the Kingdom of God, where, in the science of the blessed, God and all things are perfectly known, so far as God has willed and the light of glory enables the blessed to understand. But here in this world, in proportion as our faith is perfect, in proportion as we are illuminated with the knowledge of faith, in that proportion we shall love and adore the One God, the Ever-blessed Trinity, Jesus the Incarnate Word, His Blessed Mother, and all His Saints, and all the operations and works of His divine Kingdom upon earth. In the measure of our knowledge all these things will be the objects of devotion.

Let us sum up what I have said in this way. You all know, at least by name, the great book which, next after the Holy Scriptures, the Church has always held in veneration, the *Sum of Theology*, by the Angelic Doctor S. Thomas Aquinas. And I daresay many of you possess a small book of devotion, beautiful almost beyond compare, called the *Paradise of the Christian Soul*. Take and set that book by the side of the theology of S. Thomas, and you will find it to be dogma kindled into devotion, the commentary of love and worship upon the science of God and His Saints, beginning with the Ever-blessed Trinity, passing on to the Incarnation, from the Incarnation to the Communion of Saints, and to the presence of our Divine Lord in the Holy Eucharist. All the dogmas of faith are in that book of prayer and praise made one by one an object of devotion. Here, then, is the relation between devotion and dogma. You see, therefore, why it is that the Catholic Church, from the beginning, has been inflexibly firm in maintaining every jot and tittle of its dogma. It is because God has revealed it, and because God has committed it to its custody; because if one jot or one tittle were lost, then the Church of God would lose some object of its devotion. The whole revelation of God,—of the Ever-blessed Trinity, of the Father, the Son, and the Holy Ghost, of the Maker and the Redeemer and the Sanctifier; the mysteries of the one uncreated nature and of the three consubstantial, co-equal, co-eternal Persons; of the glory of God, of the mutual knowledge and love of Father, Son, and Holy Ghost,—this is the first great and divine reality, the object of our divine worship. To know and to adore the Ever-blessed Trinity is to adore God 'in spirit and in truth.' Next, the Incarnation of·the Son of God: the two whole and perfect natures of Godhead and Manhood united in one only Divine Person, the Godhead assuming our humanity, the humanity deified by assumption into God—our manhood become the Manhood of God; the Precious Blood, the Blood of God, which redeemed the world; the Sacred Heart, the Heart of God, which loves us with an infinite love, because it is divine: all this is to be worshipped with the divine adoration due to the Eternal Word. Here is a manifold dogma, from which the Catholic Church has never suffered the diminution of an iota. All through the first centuries of its history heretics assailed the Ever-blessed Trinity and the Incarnation of the Son. The Church stood in its majestic immobility, like the light that never wavers, casting off to the right and to the left the erroneous conceptions and the false doctrines of men. Again, because the Son of God is man, and because the Infant born in Bethlehem was a Divine Person, the Immaculate Mary was declared to be the Mother of God: infinitely below God, because she is a creature;

immensely above all creatures, because she is the Mother of God; her dignity exceeding that of all the creatures that God has ever·made; her union with Him the closest that can be conceived, save only the union of Godhead and Manhood in the one Person of her Divine Son; her sanctity surpassing that of all the creatures of His hands: immaculate in her conception, and sanctified with an immensity of grace. Here is a dogma, and from this the Catholic Church has never suffered one hair's-breadth of deviation. Again, the Communion of Saints, the mystical Body of Christ, the Head and the members; the intercommunion between earth and heaven, between the Church that is visible here in warfare and the Church that is triumphant beyond the grave; the intercession of the Saints on high, the invocation of their prayers by us on earth,—these again are dogmas; they are the outlines of divine realities. Once more, the institution of the mystery of the Ever-blessed Eucharist, the Real Presence of the Body and Blood of Jesus Christ in the Sacrament of the Altar, the true and proper and propitiatory Sacrifice of the Holy Mass,—all these things, again, are dogmas; they are divine facts, divine realities, and therefore objects of our love.

And, lastly, the divine order of the Holy Catholic Church, of which the Incarnate Son is Head at the right hand of His Father, and His Vicar, or His visible representative, is Head on earth; one, as He is one, numerically and absolutely; undivided and incapable of division, as the living body of a man, quickened by one life, from which if any member be cut off that member dies, but the body still lives on; that one Church of God, imperishable to the end of time, because the Head in heaven is Eternal Life, and the Holy Ghost is the Lord and Life-giver: infallible, both in knowledge and in utterance, because He dwells in it, and because the Spirit of Truth for ever guides it; because the illumination of the Day of Pentecost has never been overcast; for the noontide light of the revelation of God has stood still in all its splendour, without change or shadow, from that hour to this—all this is dogma, radiating from the one revealed truth of God, expressed in words chosen by divine assistance. You confess all this in the Apostles' Creed, which you repeat day by day. We say it in the Nicene Creed in the Holy Mass, and in the Athanasian Creed, which we love more and more in these last days, because the world has risen up against it, and men of faint heart are for letting it go. All these things are dogmas. They are the truths and realities of God's Kingdom, for which the Church has contended all along the line of its history in one ceaseless conflict. The war began with the Ever-blessed Trinity, and is carried on every day now against the infallibility of the Head of the Church. And between these two extremes there never has been a moment when one or more, sometimes all, the doctrines of the Holy Catholic Faith have not been in controversy. They are the cause of conflict between the world and the Church of God; but the Church has stood firm and immovable, never making any compromise; never, for the sake of gaining even a nation, departing from a single jot or tittle of the truth. If it could gain the conversion of a whole people by the cession of an iota of truth, it would refuse to cede it. Why is it so inflexible? or, as the world says, why is it so extreme? Because on the dogma of truth depends all divine worship and all devotion of the heart. What is the adoration of the Ever-blessed Trinity but the nearest approach which we here can make to the vision of God? We see and adore Him by faith. What is the adoration of the Incarnate Word in the tabernacle but the worship we shall give when we see Him as He is? You bow down at the Holy Mass, because you know

He is there. You adore Him in the Holy Sacrifice, because you know that the Oblation which He offered upon Calvary is there continued and applied to you. When the Blessed Sacrament is upon the altar you bow down before It, because you know It is the Presence of Jesus Himself; and when It is lifted up in Benediction you kneel for His blessing, as if He lifted up His hands upon His disciples. When you receive Him in Holy Communion, and go back in silence to your place, giving thanks that He has come into your soul,—these are divine realities. Speak them, and they are dogmas. Dogmas are truths, and truths are divine; for they are the mind and actions of God Himself. The world scornfully calls these things dogmas, because it does not believe in a Divine Teacher or a Divine Presence. But we know these things to be realities of the Kingdom of God; and therefore we say, 'You adore that which you know not; we adore that which we know.'

Now let me draw a picture before you. Three hundred years ago, in every country in Europe, there were cathedrals, abbeys, minsters, churches, and sanctuaries consecrated to the worship of the Ever-blessed Trinity; and in those cathedrals and abbeys and minsters and churches there were altars of the

Blessed Sacrament and of the Blessed and Immaculate Mother of God, and altars of the Saints, setting forth to us visibly the dogmas we have been reciting. There was then no jangling or controversy about the articles of faith, for all men believed the same thing; all worshipped at one altar, as the children of a common family and sons of a common Father. They had one Lord, and they were disciples of one Divine Teacher. Days they were of sweetness and peace and unity, in which the old prepared themselves to die in the full confidence that the transit from this world to the world unseen was a gentle passage from mortality to life eternal, up the luminous path which faith laid open before them; when too the little children in our green hamlets and in the woodlands of England and in their lowly cottages had the beads of our Blessed Mother in their hands. They learned dogma from their infancy without knowing it, the dogma of the five joyful mysteries and of the five sorrowful and the five glorious mysteries of Mary, in which is contained the whole revelation of God Incarnate; they assembled, day by day and week by week, before the altar of the humble parish church, to pray together as one flock, in one fold, under one Shepherd. A sweet vision of peace, but how shattered and gone! Where is it now ?   Look to Germany, in which the riot and the rout began, in which the first false apostles arose : it had not then been afflicted with the desolation of its Thirty Years' War ; it was fertile and peaceful. And what came afterwards ?   Heresy, bloodshed, civil war, the betrayal of brother by brother, a multitude of sorrows ; a reign of death, famine, pestilence, the utter wreck of nations, which stamped upon Germany deep and indelible scars, visible to this hour. From what did it all come ?   Because the unity of the faith had been destroyed, heresy began to make havoc of its people, unity of worship was broken down, and therefore unity of charity was shattered to pieces.   Men began to rise against each other in contentious strife of tongues ; they ended in bloodshed.   What is it now ?   Look at that land in which the first apostle of the new Gospel arose. We are told that, in the chief city of that people, not two men in a hundred enter a place of worship.   What belief in the dogmas of Christianity remains ?   The Christian Revelation itself has been rejected !   What belief remains in the Holy Scriptures as an inspired book ? Here and there one may believe it.   In that land, the first-born of the Reformation, which first broke the unity of faith and worship, dogma and devotion and Christianity itself are gone down into the outer darkness. At this day the special animosity of these men is directed against the Sacred Heart and all who adore it. I have no will to say anything which shall have even the sound of wounding any susceptibilities at home, in England. I have always said that the English people never rejected the Catholic faith: they were robbed of it. I repeat it now. The English people did they knew not what, under the pernicious guidance of bad men. But it has been almost as disastrous as if they had known what they did; for where is the unity of the faith in England now? where is unity of worship? How many sects and sub-sects and minor sects and sections over again do we not see, crumbling perpetually from the landslip which fell from the unity of the Church three hundred years ago. What a wasting away of Christian faith and Christian piety do we see round about us. Here we are, in a city of three millions. God only knows how many this day have set their foot in any place of Christian worship. All the places of worship in London would not contain more than a third of its population, nay, not a third of this teeming multitude. And where in this wilderness of sin do the other two millions wander up and down? How are they living? How will they die? This would not have been, had there not arisen in the midst of us proud bad men, who lifted up their heel against the divine authority of the Church of God; rejected its teaching, destroyed the unity of the faith, separated this island from the unity of Christendom, shut out the influx of the divine voice by which 'the truth as it is in Jesus' has been sustained from the Day of Pentecost until this hour; and by destroying faith they have made worship impossible.

And when I say these things I can never forget Ireland by our side—Ireland, poor, outcast, despised, down-trodden, hunted from field to field, from river to river, from mountain to mountain. But up in the mountain, and by the river-side, and on the lonely moss, the Holy Mass was offered; in the poor rude earth-hovels the beads of our Blessed Mother were said; out among the woods and the bogs the Sacraments of Penance and of Holy Communion were given; and dogma and devotion have lived on, fervent and imperishable.

Devotion thus preserves dogma, as dogma generates and quickens devotion. Let us come back to England. Is there, then, no perfect faith, no perfect worship among us? Yes; God be praised. Half a century ago it was, indeed, out of sight. For three hundred years the Holy Mass was said in the Catacombs. To-day it is visible and audible : it may be seen and it may be heard. It is in this place, it is throughout England, in all the churches and sanctuaries, where the whole dogma of faith which England received from S. Gregory the Great through its first Archbishop of Canterbury is still inviolate. The faith of the Apostle of England, undiminished in jot or tittle, has descended as our heirloom from century to century ; and with it the whole Christian worship, and all its constellation of devotions to the Sacred Humanity, to the Five Sacred Wounds, to the Most Precious Blood, to the Sacred Heart,—all these have come down as a stream of light mingled with fire in the midst of England. Here, in the midst of all the confusions and conflicts which are perpetually surging round about; debates in the highest places of this land how divine worship is to be regulated; controversies between the chief pastors,—so the Law runs,—of the English people and those who ought to be their docile sons, as to what is to be worshipped, and how,—in the midst of all this, the altar of the true Tabernacle stands immovable, and the Lamb of God is daily offered in the beauty and silence of Eternal Truth. I have no desire to dwell on these things. They are profoundly mournful : the just chastisement of a great revolt ;

the humiliation of human error once set up in pride, now with its face upon the earth. Let me therefore sum up all that I have said.

The Sacred Heart is the key of the Incarnation; the Incarnation is the treasure-house in which are all the truths of the Father, Son, and Holy Ghost. The Incarnation casts off two rays of light: on the one side, the mystery of the Holy Sacrifice of the Altar; on the other, the devotion due to the Blessed Mother of God. Any one who knows the Sacred Heart aright will know, as I said in the beginning, the whole science of God and the whole science of man, and the relations between God and man and between man and man. These truths are the dogma of dogmas, the treasures hid in the Sacred Heart, the tabernacle of God.

Make yourselves, then, disciples of the Sacred Heart; learn to know it, and that knowledge will never pass away. Faith will pass into vision, but dogma is eternal; dogma is the truth impressed upon the intelligence by faith. The obscurity of faith will pass into the light of vision; but that impression of the truth upon the glorified intelligence will abide for ever when Truth Himself shall be seen face to face.

Love, then, the Sacred Heart, and that love will

pass into the Beatific Union ;. for charity is eternal, and the love of the Sacred Heart is the union of our faint weak charity with the fervent charity, divine and human, of Jesus Christ our Lord. Adore the Sacred Heart, and it will pass into the worship of the eternal throne, where there will be prayer no longer, and reparation no more; but praise for ever, and thanksgiving to all eternity.

Do not think that the science of the Sacred Heart is too deep for you. It is the science of the poor and the science of the little child; they, by an infused light and by an implicit knowledge, know the Sacred Heart even more perfectly and more precisely than the cultivated intellect which, in its cultivation, is cold. Therefore it is a science within the reach of all; and it comes more by love than by light, more by prayer than by study; most of all it comes by communion with the Precious Body and Blood of Jesus Himself.

Make yourselves, then, disciples of His Sacred Heart. Learn to love and to be like it; and in the measure in which you are like it you will know it; and in the measure in which you know it, you will love it; and it will be in you as rest and sweetness and light and strength. You will walk with Jesus in this world as the two disciples walked with Him to Emmaus, but your eyes will not be holden: and your heart will burn within you as He talks with you by the way; and when you see Him in eternity He will not vanish out of your sight, but you will ' see Him as He is,' and He will abide with you for ever.

IV.

THE SCIENCE OF THE SACRED HEART.

THE SCIENCE OF THE SACRED HEART.

That Christ may dwell by faith in your hearts: that being rooted and founded in charity, you may be able to comprehend with all the Saints what is the breadth and length and height and depth. To know also the charity of Christ, which surpasseth all understanding, that you may be filled unto all the fulness of God. Ephes. iii. 17-19.

WE have seen that the knowledge of the Sacred Heart is the most perfect of dogmas: that it contains in itself the knowledge of God, the knowledge of man, the knowledge of the sanctification of our humanity in Jesus Christ, and therefore of our own sanctification. It sets before us an example of all perfection, and of our relations to God and to one another. We have seen also that the love of the Sacred Heart is the most perfect devotion: that it contains in itself the love of God and the love of Jesus, a tender and intimate friendship of heart with heart, the nearest union of God and man possible in this world. And we have seen also that where perfect dogma is found, perfect devotion springs from it, that these two are united as light and heat are united together, and that as the light is more intense the heat is more ardent. Light and heat may, indeed, in the spiritual world be parted; for it is possible for a man to be illuminated in the intellect and yet be cold in the heart; but to this we shall come presently. Now this appears to be what S. Paul was asking of God for the Ephesians, whom he had brought into the faith. He had for two whole years dwelt in Ephesus and taught the Ephesians everything that it was in the power of a human teacher to deliver. He was an Apostle chosen in a special manner, called by the Holy Ghost, converted by a vision of our Lord Himself, illuminated in a singular degree, and caught up into the third heaven, so that he had learnt things which it is not lawful for man to utter; nevertheless even he, after all his labour, and after delivering to the Ephesians 'the whole counsel of God,' having 'kept back nothing from them,' as he himself declares, prayed for an illumination and a knowledge which he could not bestow, which God alone could give. He prayed that their hearts might be illuminated, and that they might perceive the indwelling of Christ in their hearts by faith; that they might be 'founded and rooted in charity,' and that they might 'be able to comprehend with all the Saints what is the breadth and length and height and depth, and to know the charity of Christ, which surpasseth all understanding.' It is clear, therefore, that there is a kind of knowledge altogether supernatural, altogether a divine gift, something which is superadded, after all that we can learn by the intellect, and after all that we believe by faith. And to this we will turn our thoughts.

It seems then, from these words of the Apostle, that there are five degrees of this knowledge of Jesus, or, we may say, that there are five ways by which we know, or there are five ascents which we must make, going from step to step upwards into the light, the knowledge, and the love of the Sacred Heart. I will now endeavour, as well as I can, to point out these five degrees. But I feel that we are entering on a region —I may say on regions which are far beyond any I would profess to have trodden myself; nevertheless a teacher must teach even those things which he dare not think that he himself has yet made his own.

1. The first way of knowledge and the first beginning of the knowledge of the Sacred Heart of our Divine Lord is by the intellect illuminated by faith. The virtue of faith is supernatural, and consists in this: it is a light of the Holy Ghost infused into the

intellect, whereby the truths of revelation and the objects of faith are made, I may say, visible; so that by the vision of faith we know the truths and objects that are revealed. It has been argued among the theologians of the Church whether, in that infused light of faith, the very articles or truths of the creed are infused. Some have believed that, as in the reason of every child there is the whole power of numbers, so that a child can count as soon as it is conscious; and as soon as it comes to the age of reason the power of calculation may be elicited and trained into the most abstruse process of numbers; so also with the power of faith. They have thought, in like manner, that the mysteries of faith lie hid in the infused grace of faith; and that just as between the natural eye and the natural world there is a certain affinity, and it needs only the light of day to render the natural world visible to the faculty of sight, so with the truths of revelation and the gift of faith : that they have an affinity with each other, and that it needs only the proposition of the Church to render them visible. Every one, therefore, who is born again has this knowledge of the Sacred Heart of Jesus by the light of faith. So long as we are in a state of grace, faith works by charity and unites us by love to the

Heart of our Lord; so long as there is love, so long there is a light both of faith and charity. But by one mortal sin the charity of God is lost, the sanctifying grace of the Holy Ghost is forfeited. Charity departs with sanctifying grace, but there remain behind hope and faith; the light is still in the soul, but the love has departed. And it is of this state that a Saint has said, ' *O miserum, intellectum habere in cœlo, voluntatem in cœno,*—O miserable state, to have the intellect in heaven and the will in the mire;' that is, by the light of faith to know God and the mysteries of God, and to have the will and the heart sunk in the mire of sin. This is the divorce of light and love, which borders on the state which theologians call the faith of devils, for ' the devils believe, and tremble.' Hell itself is light without love—light to know God, to know the Ever-blessed Trinity, to know the Incarnation, to know the mysteries of Redemption when it is all too late, when salvation is impossible. Light without love turns into malice, hatred, rebellion, and remorse; the inextinguishable light of the knowledge of God in hell breeds ' the worm that never dies.' But so long as there is the grace of charity perfecting the light of faith, there faith has a special vision of the Person of Jesus Christ our Lord. S. Bernard says, ' Whenever I hear the name of Jesus I see before me a man humble, lowly, loving, poor, merciful, pitiful, and divine ;' there is a vision of beauty and sanctity, of majesty and dignity, always before the mind of those who are illuminated by faith to know the Sacred Heart of Jesus. This, then, is the first way or degree of knowledge.

2. The second is to know the Sacred Heart by love; not only by the intellect, but by the heart; and that is by the perfection of faith unfolded and ripened by charity. Faith without charity is, as I said before, light without warmth ; faith and charity are light and warmth together; and where there is charity in the heart, the vision of faith grows always more luminous and more full of love. Just as friends, the more intimately they know one another, the more they love each other, come to have a living consciousness of each other's character; so it is with charity : it perfects the vision of faith by a personal friendship with Jesus; and as charity grows, there is a closer union between the heart of the disciple and the Sacred Heart of his Master; and where there is union there is an assimilation; for love likens the object of love to itself. They that love one another by living together grow like each other. Love identifies the souls of friends, so that

they have at last but one will; and as their wills are identified, their hearts, their affections, and their ways, and even their outward manner, their tone of voice, and their accent of speech, grow like each other. They change, as it were, into each other's likeness. We say that 'a friend is another self,' because there is a power of assimilation which is natural to love. And what is true in natural things is true in divine things; and those who love our Divine Lord and are united heart to heart with Him, as they grow in likeness grow also in knowledge; they know Him better and more intimately in the measure in which they grow more like Him, and they grow more like Him in the measure in which they know Him. This is a divine paradox, a circle returning into itself. They are changed into the same likeness; and such is the meaning of the Apostle when he says, 'We are transformed into the same image, from glory to glory, as by the Spirit of the Lord.'[1] This is why the priest, if he be worthy, is called 'another Christ'—words that are our crown if we be worthy, and our condemnation if we be not. Unless the priests of the Church have learnt by faith and by love to know their Master, unless they are changed into His likeness, unless they bear His Heart

1 2 Cor. iii. 18.

within them, unless they think His thoughts and speak His words, they are not trusty witnesses; they may even give a false witness, may teach or mislead men to believe that their Master is other than He truly is. But when they are like to their Master they are evangelists of the Sacred Heart, true witnesses of their Lord, of His love and of His truth. This, then, is the second degree of the knowledge of the Sacred Heart which comes by love.

3. The third way of knowledge is the knowledge of experience. The Psalmist says, ' Taste and see how sweet the Lord is.' Is it not strange that these two senses should here be, as it were, interchanged? How can we receive sight by tasting, or by seeing, how can we taste? Yet it is true in spiritual things that if we taste we shall see. If we have tasted that the Lord is sweet, we shall know Him by an experience distinct from faith. It is a trial that we must make each one for himself. Wherever there is friendship, in proportion as it is prolonged and matured and tried in the manifold changes and vicissitudes of life, just in that measure we grow in the knowledge of our friend. And friendship has special faculties of its own. We know how friends that are intimate with each other know each other's will without a word, know each other's judgment without asking,

know how to act and how to speak in their behalf without going to them for counsel. There is an instinct and an intuition in true friendship which forecasts and knows at once what a friend would desire. So it is in the life of a true disciple who walks uprightly and in obedience and in the love of his Divine Master. Take Abraham for an example. How did God try his fidelity? What did He command him to do? God, who spoke with Abraham as a man speaks with his friend, and who called him his friend, commanded him to offer up his son. In that He tried his trustful fidelity and his spirit of sacrifice; and in that trial Abraham learned to know God and the love of God and the mercy of God with a more perfect knowledge. He obeyed without hesitation, and was ready to offer up his only son; and by that trial he entered into a knowledge and a love of God such as he had never learned before. Again, when our Divine Lord bade the blind man go and wash in the Pool of Siloe He tried his faith; and after he had gone and washed, and his eyes were opened, he came back seeing, and he knew the Son of God. Again, S. Paul says that he was 'buffeted by an angel of Satan, a sting of the flesh'—some terrible temptation—and that he had 'besought the Lord thrice'—which need not only mean three times, but daily, continuously, and without ceasing—'that it might depart from him.' And what was the answer? 'My grace is sufficient for thee; for power is made perfect in infirmity.'[2] After that answer S. Paul knew the will and the purpose of his Lord as he had never known till then. There is a continual growth of knowledge which comes by experience, and those who live in the love of the Sacred Heart find their whole life to be full of the tokens of His love to them. The consciousness of our relation to Him turns our whole life into a personal service, and all His providence into a personal oversight and guidance. It gives a meaning and a purpose to everything that befalls us. Nothing comes by chance; nothing falls out at random; everything is ordered, even the falling of a sparrow to the earth : how much more the life of man, and all the events of it. The whole order and tissue of our life are disposed by the Hand of our Divine Lord for our trial and our sanctification ; even our very temptations are permitted that we may be chastised and sanctified, our afflictions that we may be more conformed to Him in His patience, and our privations that we may know what it is to be content with Him alone. The sorrows of life are intended to conform us to the

<hr>

[2] 2 Cor. xii. 7-9.

'Man of Sorrows.' Whatsoever comes to us is ordered or permitted; and all is overruled by Him with an intention and a purpose which becomes legible to those who know Him by experience. We, then, can understand what the Apostle meant when he said, 'I know Him whom I have trusted,' that is, in whom I have believed; 'and I am certain that He is able to keep that which I have committed unto Him'—and what was it? his soul, his whole being, his salvation—'against that day,'[3] the great day of judgment to come.

Now, I ask you, have you gone beyond this? Have you yet attained to the knowledge and love of the Sacred Heart by the light of faith, and by the love of your heart, and by the personal experience of your lives? Do you interpret what befalls you in your life as the overruling, watchful, and loving care of your Divine Friend? If so, you will never murmur, nor repine, nor rebel; you will never chafe against His providence. You will be content with your lot, you will be ready to thank Him for everything. If the day is fair you will bless Him, if the day is stormy you will be content with it; you will know that nothing comes amiss, that everything that befalls you, whatsoever it be, is ordered by a Heart that loves you, and by a Wisdom that cannot err.

[3] 2 Tim. i. 12.

4. But there is still another and a fourth degree of this knowledge of the Sacred Heart.

There are two kinds of theology. There is a theology, or knowledge of God, which is acquired by study and by elaborate intellectual toil, but that is the theology of Doctors. Alas for us if there were no other theology. There is another science of God, which comes not from books, but from God Himself; not from poring over learned pages, but by the infused light of the Holy Ghost. And that infused knowledge is the theology of the Saints. Perhaps you will say, ' But we are not Saints. Why do you invite us to a knowledge which is above us ?' I answer, ' The poor and the simple and little children may be Saints; for the first shall be last and the last shall be first in the Kingdom of God. It is not only those whom we account to be Saints that are so. God gives these infused lights to all that are humble, to all that are clean of heart, for " the clean of heart shall see God." ' And by an infused light of the heart they will see God in the world around them, and in all the works of God; and they will see God in the Church and in all its history, in all its fortunes, in all its sufferings, in its warfare, in its conflicts which the world counts to be defeats. God is in them all; and the clean of heart in all these things can see His Face and the power of His Hand, and the working of His Will. They can see God also in the tradition of Faith and in every letter of their baptismal Creed, and in all the luminous truths of their Catechism. These all are theology in short words and in a little book, but it is a theology which will be eternal. They see God too in the Most Holy Sacrament of the Altar; and they see Him in all their own life by an infused light which teaches them to know that they are in the hands of their Master in heaven, and that He is their Divine Redeemer who shed His Precious Blood for them; and that nothing comes which is not ordered for their sanctification and by His Will.

This is the theology which comes not by learned books. It comes down into the heart by the inspiration of the Holy Ghost. In the history of the Church some of the greatest lights that have ever been cast upon it have been shed by the humblest and most unlettered souls. Peter himself, the first Vicar of Jesus Christ, was a fisherman; and from his day onwards God has chosen humble and pure souls as the channels of His illumination. He has chosen the handmaids of His Blessed and Immaculate Mother, unlearned women, to be special channels of light even upon dogmas of Faith. S.

Catherine of Genoa wrote, as with a pen of light, upon the mystery of Purgatory: her book on the state of souls beyond the grave is an illumination visibly from the Spirit of God. S. Gertrude received light to know the Sacred Heart long before the special illumination which was given to Blessed Margaret Mary, the founder of the devotion. The venerable Mary of Agreda, in a profuse and minute exposition, has taught us the mystery of the deified humanity and the actions and passion of our Blessed Lord. No human genius could have conceived such teaching. It can be ascribed to nothing but supernatural light. Blessed Angela of Foligno tells us that one day when she went into the church she prayed for a special grace from God, and as she began to say the 'Our Father,' in a moment, she said, 'I seemed to see the " Our Father" and every word of it in so clear a light and with so new an understanding, that I marvelled how little I had known it before.' And Blessed Margaret Mary was an unlettered woman, despised and persecuted even in her own convent, thought to be a visionary, and to be beside herself, without cultivation and without theology. Nevertheless she has left behind her writings and meditations and counsels and records of the visions she received, and instructions to those

who were under her charge, full of intuitive perception of divine truth, of subtil discernment in the
spiritual life, of ardour and love and a surpassing
knowledge of the Sacred Heart.

What was the source of all this? An infused
light—the light that was shed abroad in the heart
by the Holy Ghost. Perhaps you will say, these are
all Saints. I answer that the little child may have
all these things, for ' out of the mouths of babes and
sucklings' God glorifies Himself. There have been
turning-points in the lives of Saints which have
been determined by a word spoken by a child. S.
Augustine tells us, when he was pondering upon the
truths of Christianity before he yet became Christian, that one day, when he was meditating in a
garden in profound grief and doubt, he heard, as it
were, the voice of a child saying in a neighbouring
garden, ' *Tolle lege, tolle lege,*—Take and read, take
and read.' He laid his hand upon a roll that was
beside him, and opened it, and his eyes lighted on
the words, ' Let us walk honestly as in the day;'
' Put ye on the Lord Jesus Christ.'[4] From that
moment he turned to God.

In the history of many there are turning-points
of life of this kind. You can perhaps remember when

<hr>

[4] Rom. xiii. 13, 14.

a word read in a book, or something that you heard from a preacher, or the chance whisper of a friend moved you so as nothing had ever moved you before. Now, I ask you, do you believe that it was a mere human speech or mere human voice that made you to thrill and to listen? Was it not an infused light of the Spirit of God, who is always striving with our hearts? Like the rain that falls on the barren mountain, His grace had been flowing down into our hearts for years without leaving a change behind; but upon some one day, in some brief moment, one word was changed by an infused grace into a ray of light which pierced your understanding, and into a spark of fire which kindled the love of God in your heart.

Here, then, is another way in which we may come to know the Sacred Heart of Jesus. And these things are not beyond the reach of any of you. Any humble docile soul, by prayer and Holy Communion and kneeling before the Altar, may be ever receiving fuller illumination to know and to understand the Sacred Heart with a growing intimacy and a more ardent love. Our Lord Himself has promised it: 'I confess to Thee, O Father, Lord of heaven and earth, because Thou hast hid those things from the wise and prudent, and hast revealed them unto little ones'—that is, to children, to the docile, to the humble and the clean of heart—'yea, Father, for so hath it seemed good in Thy sight.'[5]

5. There still remains the last, a fifth, way of knowledge; and that is by the manifestation of Himself. Hear His own words: 'He that hath My commandments and keepeth them, he it is that loveth Me; and he that loveth Me shall be loved of My Father, and I will love him, and will manifest Myself to him.'[6] Now, before I venture to interpret these words, I ask you to say to yourselves, 'What do these words mean? What have I understood them to mean?' You have read these words a thousand times. Have you attached any meaning at all to them? And, if you have, what is that meaning? 'I will manifest Myself to him.' Is it to the eye, or is it to the ear, or is it by a vision, or by a voice, or by anything that is seen, or by anything that is palpable? Answer in your own hearts. First of all, no doubt our Divine Lord in these words promised that all who loved Him, and all who were faithful to Him, should see Him manifested again after He rose from the dead. He came visibly and palpably into the midst of them; S. Thomas put his finger into the print of the nails; they ate and drank

[5] S. Matt. xi. 25, 26.   [6] S. John xiv. 21.

with Him; they saw that He was the very same who had been crucified.   By the sea of Tiberias they all sat round Him, and they ate of the broiled fish and the bread which He gave to each : they knew that it was their Divine Master.   On the mountain they conversed with Him, and while He lifted up His hands and blessed them, He visibly ascended up into heaven.   This, then, may be the first fulfilment of the promise.   Afterwards, when Stephen was stoned, as he yielded up the ghost, he saw heaven opened and Jesus standing at the right hand of God.[7]   Once more.   Saul, on the way to Damascus, to persecute the disciples of Jesus, was struck down by an overwhelming light from heaven, and he saw that 'Just One,'[8] he saw Jesus Himself manifested; and again he says that, when he was called before the tribunal of the Emperor in Rome, 'At my first answer no man stood with me, but all forsook me : may it not be laid to their charge.   But the Lord stood by me and strengthened me.'[9]   This too was a manifestation of his Divine Master.   All these things are recorded in the New Testament, and you believe them.   Then, I ask you, why should not men believe what we read in the history of the Church, that when Peter was fleeing from Rome, to escape from persecution, our

<hr>

[7] Acts vii. 55.   [8] Ib. xxii. 14.   [9] 2 Tim. iv. 16, 17.

Divine Lord met him? Peter asked, 'Lord, whither art Thou going?' And Jesus said, 'I go to Rome, again to be crucified.' These words turned Peter back to win the crown of martyrdom. I ask you whether you believe it or disbelieve it. It is written in history. It is intrinsically credible. If any man disbelieves it, not upon defect of evidence, but as intrinsically incredible, he convicts himself at least of the incredulity which says that these things happened only in the time of the Holy Scriptures. Why should the same things be credible then and incredible now? I would ask, Do you believe that the dispensation of grace, and of the divine operations of the Church on earth, and the visible manifestations of our Divine Lord have ceased because they have not been recorded by inspired writers? Because we have not a continuous history of these things, a canon of Scripture reaching through eighteen hundred years, do you believe that the things themselves have ceased to be? If you see a planet sometimes obscured by a cloud, sometimes reappearing, do you doubt that the light is one and the same? Or if you see a river bury itself in the earth, and, after a long track, reappear and break up again and again above the surface, would you disbelieve its identity because you cannot trace the whole of its course? So is it with these supernatural manifestations. The whole order of the Church is supernatural. We read in the Life of S. Thomas of Canterbury that, as he was in thanksgiving after his Mass in the chapel of S. Stephen, in the Abbey of Pontigny, our Divine Lord appeared to him and called him by name. S. Thomas said, 'Who art Thou, Lord?' and He answered, 'I am Jesus, thy brother. My Church shall be glorified in thy blood, and thou shalt be glorified in Me.' Is this incredible to you? But the other day, in the East, in Corea, a humble native Christian, whose baptismal name was Charles, as he returned from Pekin, twice saw in a dream, as he declared, our Divine Lord, who said to him, 'In the course of this year I will give thee the grace of shedding thy blood for the glory of My name.'[10] He returned home fully possessed with the belief that his martyrdom was close at hand. Soon after, the persecution broke out and he was martyred. Why doubt these things? You do not doubt that the Holy Ghost, who came on the Day of Pentecost, is here. You cannot see Him, you see no tongues of fire, you hear no sound of the thrilling wind, and yet you believe in the perpetual operation of God the Holy

---

[10] *The New Glories of the Catholic Church*, p. 65 (Richardson, 1870).

Ghost. Believe, then, in the perpetual promise of our Divine Lord: 'He that loveth Me shall be loved of My Father, and I will love him, and will manifest Myself to him.' What is the life of Blessed Margaret Mary, chosen to be the channel of the devotion to the Sacred Heart, but one continual evidence of this wonderful and luminous manifestation of His presence? He gave her seventy visions of Himself—seventy times, in supernatural ways, He manifested to her this devotion of the Sacred Heart in its light and in its love. These things are things of the Kingdom of God, supernatural indeed, because they are above nature, but I was going to say natural, because the Kingdom of God itself is divine, and all its laws are supernatural. But perhaps you will say that you do not look for these manifestations. No, nor do I. But I do believe that to you and to me our Lord does manifest Himself. And how? Not palpably, it may be, as He did after the Resurection; not visibly, as He did to S. Thomas of Canterbury and the Blessed Margaret Mary; but invisibly, yet personally and truly and inwardly, every time we make a worthy Communion. And in the measure in which we live in communion with Him, in the degree in which we are pervaded by the consciousness that we are united to His Sacred Heart, He will manifest

Himself to us.   We know that which we cannot see, and we taste that which we cannot touch.   We know that He is with us, for He Himself hath said, 'He that eateth My flesh and drinketh My blood abideth in Me and I in him.'[11]   If He abide in us, how is He not manifest to us ?

We have here, then, five ways of knowledge—by the intellect, by the heart, by experience, by the infused grace of the Holy Ghost, and by His inscrutable manifestations, which, to such as you and me, are invisible and spiritual, but nevertheless personal, real, and true.

If, then, you would learn to know the Sacred Heart, you must learn it of Itself.   Books will not teach it to you, and preachers cannot.   You must learn it from Him who alone can teach the heart. The Master of that doctrine sits at the right hand of God, and Jesus alone can lead you on from step to step to know and to love Him in the five ways which I have endeavoured to trace.   It begins with a secret infused grace of faith; it ends with the manifestation of Himself.   And there are two chief ways in which He teaches us to know the science of His Sacred Heart : the one is by a docile submission to His divine Voice, speaking through His Church.

[11] S. John vi. 57.

There is no other channel of His Truth, there is no other witness of His Revelation, there is no other teacher from whom we can learn His divine and unerring will. Therefore, to listen to the voice of His Church with the docility of children, and to learn the whole dogma of the Godhead and manhood of His Incarnate Person, is the first condition of the knowledge and love of the Sacred Heart. The other way is upon the altar—the Most Holy Sacrament—in which and from which His attractions are perpetually going forth, as the virtues went out from His garment upon earth, fulfilling His words: 'And I, if I be lifted up from the earth, will draw all things to Myself.'[12] There comes an illumination, and what I may call an articulate voice, from the silence of Jesus in the Blessed Sacrament, by which He teaches all those who do not hinder His light.

Worldliness is like the dust which darkens the sight of the eye. 'Love not the world, nor the things which are in the world. If any man love the world, the charity of the Father is not in him. For all that is in the world is the concupiscence of the flesh, and the concupiscence of the eyes, and the pride of life, which is not of the Father, but is of the world.'[13] And they that have these clouds in them cannot know

[12] S. John xii. 32.   [13] 1 S. John ii. 15, 16.

and love the Sacred Heart. And I must add that levity, carelessness, shallowness of heart, hinder the entrance of His light. Some people have not sufficient gravity or earnestness to understand divine truth. No hearts are more blind than the light and careless.

Therefore open your hearts wide, be candid as the day. 'If thine eye be single, thine whole body shall be full of light; if thine eye be double, thine whole body shall be full of darkness. If, then, the light that is in thee be darkness, how great shall that darkness be.'[14] Be perfectly sincere and upright with our Divine Master; let there be no false surrenderings of the heart, no secret reservations, keeping anything in yourselves back from His service. Cut off the right hand, pluck out the right eye, if they stand between you and your fidelity to Him. Out of generosity He gave the last drop of His Blood for you, keeping nothing back from you : so be and so do for Him in turn.

In this way, if you do not reach the highest degrees of knowledge, you will at least be ascending up that ladder of which the foot is on earth and the head in heaven. It reaches the Sacred Heart itself; and in them who go up by these degrees of know-

[14] S. Matt. vi. 22, 23.

ledge and love shall be fulfilled the words of our
Lord: 'I am the gate: by Me, if any man shall
enter in, he shall be saved; and he shall go in and
he shall go out, and he shall find pasture.'[15]

[15] S. John x. 9.

V.

THE LAST WILL OF THE SACRED HEART.

THE LAST WILL OF THE SACRED HEART.

With desire I have desired to eat this Pasch with you before I
suffer. S. Luke xxii. 15.

I HAVE hitherto spoken of the Sacred Heart as the
interpretation of the mystery of God Incarnate; and
next, as the centre of all doctrine, and therefore as
the source of all devotion; and lastly, we have seen
the ways in which we come to know, and therefore
to love, the Sacred Heart. We have now to consider
the character of our Divine Lord as it is manifested
in the Sacred Heart.

I have said that there are two ways by which our
Divine Lord teaches us to know and to love Him.

The first way by which He teaches us to know His
Sacred Heart is the living voice—divine, and therefore unerring—of the only Church of God. That living voice, by its articulate and infallible utterance,
teaches us the knowledge of the doctrines of faith,
and makes them definite and certain in our intellect.

The other way whereby we come to the love of the Sacred Heart is, as I have said, the Most Holy Sacrament of the Altar. Now we will take this latter point ; and my purpose will be to show how the Most Holy Sacrament is a revelation of His character.

I can find no more explicit words in proof of what I have said than those which I have taken from the lips of our Divine Lord in the Gospel of S. Luke. He said, ' With desire I have desired'— that is, by a Hebrew reduplication of the words, I have intensely desired—' to eat this Pasch with you before I suffer.' That last Paschal Supper was a time to which He had looked with an intense longing. In one word, it was at that time and in that place and in that night when He was betrayed that our Divine Lord instituted this Most Holy Sacrament of His love. It is the revelation of His love to us. It is more; it is the perpetual application of His love to our salvation. It is also the object of His love, and it ought therefore to be the object of our love in return. This is the point to which I wish to call your thoughts.

Let us, then, consider what were the reasons why our Divine Lord so intensely desired to partake of that Paschal Supper.

1. First, because it was the end of His sorrows.

His whole life on earth was one continuous sorrow—
a ceaseless sorrow that was growing in volume and
intensity for the thirty-three years of His life.   The
sorrows of our Divine Lord began from the first
moment of His Incarnation.   In that same instant
the deified soul of Jesus had its full capacity.   It
was not in a state of imperfect development; it was
not in a condition of unconsciousness, in which future knowledge was to be infused or acquired little
by little; but from the beginning, when the human
soul was assumed by the Son of God, in that moment
it entered fully and altogether into a complete knowledge of the life that was before it.   In that moment
He foresaw the whole future of His life and death;
in that moment the human intelligence, deified by
assumption into God, foreknew the whole Passion
that was to come; and by divine and human knowledge knowing the sorrow that He was to enter
upon, He deliberately, by a divine choice, and by the
consent of His human will, for the redemption of
the world, made that life of sorrow His own.   And
therefore the sorrows of the Son of God were like
ours indeed, because they were human sorrows; but
they were not like ours in this, that He foresaw them
all; but ours we do not foresee.   Through the whole
of our life He, in His mercy, hides from us the

things that we shall have to endure—the many trials, the pains, the afflictions of our lives are hid from us until they come. If we ever foresee them, it is only little by little, and as they approach us. But He saw all before Him. And we know that the suffering is increased by the clearness and the distinctness with which we foresee the sufferings that are to come. When we foresee them we suffer them twice over—once in foresight and once in reality. And therefore, in His mercy He has ordained that our foresight of sorrows should be but little. He withholds it till the moment of suffering is come; and when that moment comes He gives us strength to endure it. Not so with Himself. He foresaw through His whole life the future before He suffered, and therefore in this way He suffered twice all the griefs and sufferings of His life. At last, when that night of the Paschal Supper was come, His sorrows were at the full, and He knew that the turn in the tide was near. The flood was at its height, and it was about to ebb. He had sorrowed for three-and-thirty years, and He was come to the time when His Passion should be accomplished, and He should sorrow no more. He had foreseen that last night; He had foreseen the sadness of that last meeting and of that last farewell. He had foreseen all the circumstances of His Passion; His betrayal by a friend who was false; His betrayal by a kiss, the token of a love which was still more false. He had foreseen all the agonies in the garden under the shade of the olive-trees—all that night of buffeting and scoffing and scourging and mockery. He had looked forward to all these things, and had said, 'I have a baptism wherewith I am to be baptised, and how am I straitened until it be accomplished.'[1] To the traitor He said, 'What thou dost do quickly;'[2] meaning that He had an intense desire to enter into that last conflict, and that the last conflict should be over. Here, then, was the first reason : it was the thirst of the Sacred Heart to suffer for us—an intense desire for the redemption of the world, and a sinless impatience for the end of His sorrow unto death.

2. But, once more, the night of that Last Supper was a time full of sadness, but full of sweetness too. It was full of sadness, because the hour of His Passion was come. It was full of sweetness, because He was for the last time gathered with those whom He loved. He was there with His disciples, with those friends, weak and ignorant, and yet loving and fast, who had cleaved to Him for three long years, through evil report and good report, through shame

<hr>

[1] S. Luke xii. 50.   [2] S. John xiii. 27.

and through danger. Many had gone back from Him, but they had remained faithful. He was sitting in the midst of them, and interchanging with them the tokens of their mutual love. John lay upon His bosom, and the others were conversing with Him. He was speaking to them of a coming trial, and He said, 'Because I have said these things sorrow has filled your heart. Let not your hearts be troubled.' 'You shall lament and weep, but the world shall rejoice; and you shall be made sorrowful, but your sorrow shall be turned into joy.'[3] And when He began to speak of going away their hearts were more deeply troubled; and He consoled them under that sudden fear, saying, 'In My Father's house there are many mansions,' 'I will come again,' and 'I will not leave you orphans: I will come to you.'[4] And they gazed upon one another like men who feel that the shadow of some great change is sensibly falling upon them. They were already sorrowful, but they had forebodings of some greater sorrow yet to come. Such moments have a strange sweetness even in their sadness and fear. For it was as the time of a last farewell; and farewells are sad indeed, but sweet beyond all words. You have known it, when friends bid farewell to go into far-off

---

[3] S. John xiv. 1, xvi. 20.　　　[4] Ibid. xiv. 2.

lands, perhaps never to meet again; how they watch together through the long last night, and converse with one another until the sun rises: and those last hours, though they are overcast by the shadow of a parting so soon to come, have nevertheless a sweetness that no time in all their memory can surpass. The recollection of those last hours is treasured up through life for ever. Or you may have known it in parting from mother, or sister, or brother, when you were taking a last farewell; how, in those last moments, some token of love has been given to you, the least memorial of the past—it may be a book, or a flower dried within its leaves, or something that they have familiarly used—which will for ever recall their presence. And if in that moment they have given you the expression of a wish, a word would be a commandment which you would obey for ever. Though they had given only a sign of their will, that will would be a command which you would obey to the end of life. It was in such an hour that Jesus took bread and blessed it, and brake it and gave it to them, and said, 'Do this for a commemoration of Me.' It was the command of that dying love, the last commandment, I may say, that He ever gave in memory of Himself; the token of His dying love, to be the memorial of it and the test of ours in return. And therefore it is that the Church of God every morning commemorates the Passion of its Divine Head ; and therefore it is the faithful, with loving hearts, love the Holy Mass. It was in that last hour of the Paschal Supper that Jesus instituted that Most Holy Sacrament; to be to us the last will and testament of His Sacred Heart.

3. Again, in that hour and in that action He offered up the Lamb that was slain from the beginning of the world. The atoning Sacrifice predestined from all eternity was then offered up. The true Lamb was there. The types and the shadows passed away, the reality was come. Jesus, without spot or blemish, the Lamb immaculate and holy, was brought up into the courts of the Temple. From the first moment of the Incarnation the Son of God assumed His eternal priesthood; the Divine Infant was the Priest of the order of Melchisedech, the great High-Priest of the whole human race, who makes atonement for the sin of the world. In the moment of the Incarnation He was consecrated : He assumed His sacerdotal vestments, and put upon Him the stole of His priesthood. The three-and-thirty years of His life were sacerdotal—a life of self-oblation, of reparation, and of atonement. He was not only Priest, but Victim : He was a sacrifice

all through His life; and what was that sacrifice? It was what, in the spirit of prophecy, He had declared: ' Sacrifice and oblations and holocausts for sin Thou wouldst not.' ' In the head of the book it is written of Me, Behold, I come to do Thy will, O God.'[5] The sacrifice was the life-long oblation of His will. It was the oblation of His perfect will in perfect obedience and perfect patience even unto death. This it was that redeemed the world. And from all eternity this oblation was accepted; and from the beginning of the world this sacrifice was foreseen; and for the merits of this sacrifice all the inspirations and effusions of grace that have saved mankind, before He came, were given.

In this last Paschal Supper, when Jesus sat at the table, and took bread, blessed it, broke it, gave it, and said, ' This is My Body,' and the chalice, when He had blessed it, and said, ' This is My Blood,' He began the act of oblation, finished upon Calvary, which redeemed the world. He offered that sacrifice first without bloodshedding; but it was the same true, proper, and propitiatory sacrifice which redeems the world, because therein He offered Himself. We read in the Gospels that ' No man laid hands on Him, because His hour was not yet come;'[6] that is, no man

[5] Heb. x. 8, 9.   [6] S. John vii. 30.

had power to take Him until He delivered Himself into their hands. We read again that the servants of the high-priest who came out to seize Him in the garden of Gethsemani, when they heard Him say, 'I am He,'[7] went backward and fell to the ground — the majesty of His divine presence awed them. They were cast at His feet in fear; and in proof that, when they took Him and bound Him, it was of His own free will. When He stood before Pilate, He said once more, 'Thou shouldst not have any power against Me, unless it were given thee from above.'[8] Bound as He was, still no man had power over Him. Twelve legions of angels would have surrounded Him: they would have cut His bonds and set Him free, if it had been His divine will. Therefore at His Last Supper He made a free and voluntary offering of Himself. He had not yet shed His Blood, but throughout His whole life He had offered His will, and He now offered His death; and that which He began at the Last Supper he accomplished on the morrow upon Calvary by the shedding of Blood; for that shedding of Blood was the completion of His sacrifice. Nevertheless, when He sat at the table in the guest-chamber, He truly offered Himself, the one true, proper, and propitiatory sacrifice that takes

[7] S. John xviii. 6.   [8] Ibid. xix. 11.

away the sin of the world. The merits of the Incarnate Son were there: they were sufficient at that time to take away the sin of all mankind if it had not been His will to die. He died to complete the sacrifice, to fill up its perfect propitiation by the last gift that He could give, by the last drop of His Precious Blood.

When He said, 'This is My Body,' and 'This is My Blood,' He instituted the Holy Sacrifice; and when He said, 'This do in commemoration of Me,' He consecrated His Apostles to be priests, to offer for ever that same sacrifice of Himself. Therefore, what the Church offers, day by day, is the continuance of that same divine act which Jesus at that hour began. It is nothing new, nothing distinct from it, nothing added to it, for in itself it was perfect—a Divine Sacrifice admitting of no addition. The Sacrifice of the Altar is the same sacrifice prolonged for ever. He who offered Himself then offers Himself now. He offered Himself then by His own hands; He offers Himself now by the hands of His priesthood. There is now no shedding of blood—that was accomplished once for all upon Calvary. The action of the Last Supper looked onward to that action on Calvary, as the action of the Holy Mass looks backward upon it. As the shadow is cast by the rising sun towards the west, and as the shadow is cast by the setting sun towards the east, so the Holy Mass is, I may say, the shadow of Calvary, but it is also the reality. That which was done in the Paschal Supper in the guest-chamber, and that which is done upon the altar in the Holy Mass, is one and the same act— the offering of Jesus Christ Himself, the true, proper, propitiatory, and only Sacrifice for the sin of the world. And there, in that Holy Sacrifice of the Mass, is the Sacred Heart in all the fulness of its atonement, in all the propitiation of its Precious Blood, in all the worship and adoration of its praise and thanksgiving, in all the power of its intercession by the infinite merits of the Incarnate Son. There upon the paten and there in the chalice every morning is the Sacred Heart in all the plenitude of its redeeming power, of its infinite merits, of its unutterable love, of its exquisite tenderness for sinners. It is indeed a commemoration, because it is the perpetual visible memorial of a reality; and it is also the reality itself, because it is His Body and Blood ; that is, it is the Real Presence of Jesus, God and man. It is also the application of His Death and Passion to the souls of those who believe. The Sacred Heart, then, is there in the Holy Mass, teaching us by Itself to know His love.

4. But still further: He desired that last Paschal

Supper, because in that hour He instituted a new way of perpetual presence in the midst of us. He had promised His disciples, 'It is expedient for you that I go; for if I go not, the Paraclete will not come unto you; but if I go, I will send Him unto you.' He promised more than this. He said that He would not leave them orphans, but that He would come to them again. And He said still more: 'Behold, I am with you all days, even to the consummation of the world.' He has fulfilled this promise in many ways; but, above all, He has fulfilled it in the Holy Sacrament of the Altar. The Council of Trent,[9] in the Catechism which it puts into the hands of its priests, speaks thus: 'Jesus having loved His own while He was in the world, loved them unto the end; and now, knowing that the time was come that He should depart unto the Father, in order that He might never be absent from His own —that is, that He might never be absent from His Church —He ordained a divine and wonderful pledge of His love, and by a counsel inexplicable to us, He ac-

---

[9] 'Cum enim Dominus dilexisset suos, in finem dilexit eos: cujus quidem amoris ut divinum aliquod atque admirabile pignus daret, sciens horum jam advenisse, ut transiret ex hoc mundo ad Patrem, ne ullo unquam tempore a suis abesset, inexplicabili consilio, quod omnem naturæ ordinem et conditionem saperat, perfecit.' *Catech. Rom.* p. ii. c. iv. 2.

complished this mystery of His presence in a way that transcends the order and the conditions of nature.' The meaning is this: there are three ways in which God is present in the world. He was present from the beginning as God in a divine manner; next, He was present when He came, into the world, incarnate, in a divine and human manner; lastly, He is present now in the world, in a divine and human and a sacramental manner. He was present in the world as God from the beginning, in a divine manner; for 'all things were made by Him, and without Him was made nothing that was made; He was in the world, and the world knew Him not.' He was in the world, by His essence sustaining all things that He had made, by His presence ruling and giving laws to them all, and by His power preserving them all. And His presence in the world was luminous, not to the eyes of faith only, but to pure reason, if only the intelligence in man were not darkened by sin. Like as the sun in the heavens is luminous, resplendent, and self-evident, so the existence and the presence of God in the world would be, if men had the will to see. But there are three causes why men are blind. One is, that the light is too great—it overwhelms them; and the more light the less men see. The next is, because through their own sin the light fails

to give them light. 'They have eyes, and they see
not.' And the last is, that they darken their own
sight. They become judicially blind, like Elymas the
magician. The first presence of God in the world,
then, is in a divine manner; the next was by Incarnation, by the presence of His two natures of God
and man in one Person: it was therefore divine and
human; it included all the first and it superadded
another, and that other was a palpable and visible
presence in the midst of men, visible to their eyes
and palpable to their sense. S. John says, 'That
which was from the beginning, which we have heard;
which we have seen with our eyes; which we have
looked upon, and our hands have handled.'[10] He
came as a man born of a Virgin; He conversed
among men, He ate and drank with them, He dwelt
in the midst of them, He hungered and thirsted,
He was weary, and He wrought miracles amongst
them. He was Himself above the order and the conditions of nature, because He was the Incarnate God.
Our humanity was assumed into God. Therefore
Jesus was above the order and the condition of
nature; and being above the order of nature, He
said, 'No man hath seen God at any time, but the
Only-begotten, who is in the bosom of His Father'

[10] 1 S. John i. 1.

—at the moment He was speaking—'He hath declared Him.' 'No man hath ascended up into heaven,
save He only that came down from heaven, the
Son of Man, who, while I speak, is in heaven.'[11]
He was therefore in the world, and yet above all the
order and conditions of the world. More than this,
He had dominion over nature, being its Creator.
He had power to multiply the bread in the wilderness,
because it was the creature of His hands; He had
power to give sight to the blind, because it was
He who created the eye; He had power to restore
hearing to the deaf, because the hearing ear was
of His own making; He had power to cleanse the
leper, because He had made man, and could cleanse
the work of His own hands; He had power to walk
upon the water, because when He made the earth He
made the sea likewise; He had power to raise the
dead, because He was the Giver of life. Therefore
He was above all the conditions of nature, and had
dominion over them all, for He was God. Nevertheless, when He was in the midst of men, the Jews
thought that He was the son of a carpenter, because
they judged only by sense. Nicodemus interpreted
sense by reason. He knew that He must be a teacher
sent from God, for no man could do the miracles that

<hr>

[11] S. John iii. 13.

He did, except God were with Him. Peter knew Him to be Christ, the Son of the Living God; but not by sense alone, nor by reason alone, but by reason illuminated by faith. 'Flesh and blood hath not revealed it to thee, but My Father who is in heaven.'

But there is another way of the presence of God in the midst of us now, which is divine, human, and sacramental; and in the mystery of the altar there is Jesus, God and man, above the order and the conditions of nature, as He was when He was visible and palpable on earth. He is no longer visible and no longer palpable, because He is present under the veil of the Most Holy Sacrament.[12] According to the natural manner of existence, and in the dimensions of His human nature, He is in glory at the right hand of God; but according to the sacramental mode of His existence, which admits of neither dimensions, nor magnitude, nor locality, nor of the order or the conditions of nature, He is in the Most Holy Sacrament. He is there, as the holy Council of Trent says, not as in a place which, being circumscribed, circum-

[12] 'Neque enim hæc inter se pugnant, ut ipse Salvator noster semper ad dexteram Patris in cœlis assideat juxta modum existendi naturalem, et ut multis nihilominus aliis in locis sacramentaliter præsens sua substantia nobis adsit ea existendi ratione, quam etsi verbis exprimere vix possumus, possibilem tamen esse Deo cogitatione per fidem illustrata assequi possumus.' Conc. Trid. Sess. xiii. cap. i.

scribes all that it contains; but, being the infinite God, He is there without circumscription; there in very truth, there in reality, there as God and man, nevertheless not contained by circumscription of place, nor subject to the conditions or order of nature. You ask me how He is there. He is there as God is everywhere; and where He is in His Godhead there He is in His manhood also. How is His manhood present? It is present, as the Council of Trent says, as it is a substance.[13] The foot of a man placed upon the earth is the very reality of his presence, yet no man will say that the footprint circumscribes the man; nevertheless it is a proof that he is there. This is feeble, imperfect, and remote from the divine reality; still is enough to make this divine fact in some way comprehensible to our minds illuminated by faith. But men judge of the Most Holy Sacrament as the Jews judged of our Divine Lord's presence when they saw Him. The world, judging by sense, tells us it is bread and wine; for the men of sense have no spiritual intuition, as the Apostle has before declared of them: 'The sensual' or the animal man—that is,

---

[13] ' Christi corpus in Eucharistia non est ut in loco. Etenim locus res ipsas consequitur, ut magnitudine aliqua præditæ sunt: Christum vero Dominum ea ratione in sacramento esse non dicimus, ut magnus aut parvus est, quod ad quantitatem pertinet, sed ut substantia est.' *Catech. Rom.* p. ii. c. iv. 44.

the man of sense—' perceiveth not the things of the
spirit of God, neither can he discern them, for they
are spiritually examined'[14] or discerned.   They are
known only to the spiritual man.   A man who has
reason says, ' Under this appearance of bread and
wine there are the substances of bread and wine ;' and
he contends that the doctrine of Transubstantiation
cannot be true, because bread and wine must have
each their proper natural substance.   If, indeed, it
were in the order of nature, reason would be right ;
but the Council of Trent begins by affirming that it
is above the order and the conditions of nature.   The
bread and wine before consecration are bread and
wine, subject to the order of nature alone ; but when
consecrated by the Word of God, Who in the beginning said, ' Let the light be, and the light was,' at
His divine words, ' This is My Body, this is My
Blood,' they pass from the order of nature to the
supernatural order : they are what God calls them ;
for what He calls them, that they are thereby made.
By faith therefore illuminating reason we know this,
that what to sense is bread and wine, and what to
natural reason has natural substance, to the light of
faith, and to reason judging by faith, is the Body
and the Blood of Jesus Christ.   Therefore we say,

[14] 1 Cor. ii. 14.

in the solemn rhythm of the Church, ' on the Cross the Godhead lay hid;' but here, ' in the Most Holy Sacrament, both Godhead and manhood are hidden.' But where the manhood is, there is the Sacred Heart. Under the veil of the Most Holy Sacrament, as a vesture hanging between His presence and our sight, there is the Word Incarnate ; and out from that vesture there goes forth the virtue of healing, as it went out from the hem of His garment when the poor woman touched it visibly on earth.

5. And lastly, in that Paschal Supper He also instituted for us a new way of union with Himself. We were the children of the first Adam, and we partook of the substance of his flesh and blood ; we were of his flesh and of his bone, because we were born, according to the order of nature, unto sin and death. When, by regeneration of the Holy Ghost and by the Most Holy Sacrament of the Altar, we are made members of the second Adam, we partake of His Divine Flesh and Blood ; we are made bone of His Bone, flesh of His Flesh ; and we are partakers of His substance unto life and immortality. What is the world dreaming about when it contends with such heat and vehemence that the Sacrament of the Altar is but a representation ? Is the world content

with a shadow instead of a reality? And does it desire
to have not a reality but a shadow for its inheritance?
What does the world mean by disputing away the
Real Presence of Jesus Christ in the Most Holy Sacrament? It is a strange infatuation. If you saw a man
squandering his inheritance, you would think him to
be a fool; if you saw him casting from him precious
stones and pearls of great price, you would think him
a madman. Why, then, shall we think the world
wise in trying to persuade itself, and to persuade
others, that the Most Holy Sacrament of the Altar is
nothing but a shadow, and not a divine reality? And
if the Most Holy Sacrament of the Altar be only a
shadow, I would ask, is the Incarnation only a shadow?
There were heretics in the beginning who were called
Phantasiastæ, because they taught that the manhood
of Jesus was only an appearance. And how did the
Christians and the Martyrs of those days answer
them? They said that the Incarnation was real and
true, as the Flesh and Blood of Jesus in the Most Holy
Eucharist is real and true. They argued from the
reality of the Most Holy Sacrament to the reality of
the Incarnation. We argue from the reality of the Incarnation to the reality of His Sacramental Presence.
Nay, more. I would ask the wise men of the world,
who still call themselves Christians, do they believe

the Resurrection to be a figure or a reality ? Shall we
not rise in our own bodies ?   Shall we not be clothed
in these same bodies of ours, only glorified and im-
mortal ?   And if the Incarnation be a reality and
the Resurrection be a reality, what is the mystery of
the Most Precious Body and Blood of Jesus Christ
but the link between these two realities and the
means whereby we are made members of His substance, and thereby partakers of Him who has said,
'I am the Resurrection and the Life' ?   Therefore
our Lord has instituted the Holy Eucharist as a
means whereby we are made partakers of His very
substance.   We belong to the second Adam, as His
lineal descendants, as members and partakers of His
Flesh and of His Bone.   We are incorporated into
Him.   Hear His own words : ' Unless you eat My
Flesh and drink My Blood, you shall have no life in
you ;' and lest there should be any error, or evasion
of His meaning, He added, ' As the living Father
hath sent Me, and I live by the Father, so he that
eateth Me, even he shall live by Me.'[15] How does the
Eternal Son live by the Eternal Father, but because
the Son is consubstantial with the Father ?   And
how do we who eat the Flesh and drink the Blood of
Jesus Christ live by Him, but because we are made

[15] S. John vi. 58.

consubstantial with Him; that is, we partake of His very humanity, and that humanity is our own, deified in His Person? This is the Flesh which He gives for the life of the world, the living Bread which came down from heaven. And as we are incorporated into Him, we are made to be of one heart with Him: 'He that eateth My Flesh and drinketh My Blood abideth in Me and I in him.' He takes our heart into His Heart, and places His Heart in ours; thereby He makes us to love the things He loves, and to hate the things He hates, and to have no will but His. He dwells in those in whom His Sacred Heart abides; He makes them to be His dwelling-place; and if He dwells in them He changes them into His own likeness; He makes them to be like Himself in mind, in thought, in will, and in affection, that they may be like Him in life. There can be no external conformity to our Master if there be not first an internal transformation of the heart into His likeness. And therefore Holy Communion in the Most Precious Body and Blood of Jesus Christ is the way to know and to learn the love of the Sacred Heart to us. By receiving it into ours, and by being conformed to His likeness, we love Him again; for it is by likeness that we know, and by knowing that we love Him.

This it is that makes the unity of the Church indissoluble. In all ages, over all the world, all the action and malice of men, all the power of the gates of hell, all the audacities of heresy, all the cleavings of schism, all the seductions of false science, all the powers of the world, and all the persecutions of Satan have never been able to prevail against the indissoluble unity of the one only Church, Catholic and Roman. It is because the Sacred Heart of Jesus in the Most Blessed Sacrament is the centre of all hearts. All who are faithful are united to Him : as flames mingle with flames and the multitudes become one, so the unity, supernatural and spiritual, of all those that are united to His Sacred Heart is above the order and the conditions of nature, and the gates of hell cannot prevail against it. Shall I ask, Why is it that every other system that has pulled down the altar, rifled the tabernacle, cast off the Holy Sacrifice, denied the Real Presence,—shall I ask why it is that these systems (call them what they may), dignified by worldly wealth, by legal authority, by great learning, by social power, as they visibly are, cannot hold the souls of men together ? They crumble perpetually, they are wasting every day by a continual decay, losing on the right hand and on the left the hearts and wills which outwardly adhere to them, and are only kept together by the strong bond of worldly interest or by the imperious penalties of law. Why is it? It is because where they worship there is no lamp burning before the altar, no tabernacle, no Sacramental Presence. The Incarnate Word is not there. The centre of all unity is gone; the Sacred Heart does not dwell in the midst of them. They have rejected the Real and Sacramental Presence of Jesus Christ.

Now I have endeavoured to give the reasons why our Divine Lord so desired that Paschal night. It was the end of His sorrows; it was the hour of His last sad but sweet farewell; it was the offering of the Sacrifice that takes away the sin of the world; it began His new way of presence in the midst of us; it opened His new and intimate way of union with us for ever. Let us therefore sum up what I have been saying.

1. If any man loves our Divine Lord, he will love the Most Holy Sacrament; and ' if any man love not our Lord Jesus, let him be anathema maran atha.'[16] This is the sentence of the Apostle, and the sentence of the Apostle is the sentence of the Holy Ghost. The Most Holy Sacrament of the Altar is the presence of Jesus. It was ordained for this purpose, to keep

---

[16] 1 Cor. xvi. 22.

alive in the midst of His disciples the sense that
He is never absent; and wherever the Blessed
Sacrament is in all the world there is Jesus Christ.
It matters not whether in the guest-chamber, or
deep in the Catacombs, or on the mountain-side, or
in the forests of wild lands, in the hovels where we
in England begin our missions, or in the stately
basilicas of Rome,—there is the Blessed Sacrament,
and there is Jesus; and there is shed abroad a
sense of His presence, which pervades every place
and fills every heart; ay, even those who do not fully
believe, when they come into our sanctuaries, feel
something strange; something thrills in them, there
is a vibration in their heart, a consciousness that
they have entered into a presence that may be felt.
They do not feel it elsewhere: they cannot account
for it, they cannot deny it.   But of the stately vaults
under which the Blessed Sacrament once was, and is
no longer, what shall I say? There is in them a sense
of absence—an absence which may be felt.   All is
empty and void.   No man who has ever known the
sense of what it is to enter a Catholic church can go
into one of the ancient minsters, the noble cathedrals which the faith of our ancestors reared in
England, without saying: 'There is a sensible absence
here; some one who ought to be in this place, and

to reign in it as the Lord of the sanctuary, is here no longer. The tokens of Him who once reigned in this sanctuary speak with an almost articulate voice.' It is like our churches on Good Friday, when the altars are stripped, and the lights are out, and the tabernacle is empty and the door left open wide, that all men may know and feel ' He is not here.'

2. They who love the Blessed Sacrament love it also because it is the most intimate way of conversing with Jesus. We converse with Him in our private chamber in our prayers; we converse with Him when we pray anywhere all the day long, by the roadside, or in the throng of men. But what is that to kneeling before the Blessed Sacrament? If every day you could speak for a quarter of an hour with your angel-guardian it would leave an impression on you all the day long. S. Stephen's face shone like an angel's; so if you could stand visibly face to face with your guardian-angel for a quarter of an hour in the morning your face would shine, and people would know that you had been conversing with some bright and blessed presence higher than your own. Or if you could daily see one of the Saints—the beloved disciple, who lay upon the bosom of Jesus at Supper—if you could see him, day by day, even for a passing moment, what an impression it would leave

upon you. And yet, do you not see here the Lord of Angels and the King of Saints morning after morning in the Holy Mass? and may you not at any time come and kneel down here in His presence? and may you not converse with Him, not for a quarter of an hour only, but as long as you will? You may weary of His presence; He is never wearied of yours.

3. And once more. If you love the Blessed Sacrament, the Blessed Sacrament by its own light will teach you to know and to love the Sacred Heart; and the Sacred Heart will open itself, and will teach us to know its own character. We shall know all its love —the love which is from eternity to eternity; the love of ineffable divine fervour, of unspeakable human tenderness; the Love that died for us. We shall know too the commandment of that Love when He was about to die for us. And we shall learn not only His love, but His patience; for He abides in the midst of us for ever. Sinners as we are—cold, ungrateful, reckless, and heedless as we are— He still dwells in the midst of us in His humility, veiled, out of sight, slighted and disbelieved, passed without a sign of recognition by the multitudes that go by Him. There He is, in His generosity, giving away grace after grace. We become bankrupt through our fault and sin; we go back to Him: He restores to us the

graces that we have lost ; more than this, He pours out upon us even more grace than we have wasted, for His generosity is inexhaustible. He does not 'break the bruised reed' nor 'quench the smoking flax.' He waits for you. He has waited for you from your childhood and in your youth and in your manhood ; in all your wanderings He has been waiting for you still ; trying to draw you towards Him, that some day, at last, you may come to true repentance, and that some day before you die you may be His disciple. And in all this see what I may call His unsuspiciousness. Friends suspect one another, they form rash judgments of one another, they are always harbouring hard thoughts of each other, they draw to themselves pictures and characters of other men, and seldom in their favour. How does the Sacred Heart deal with us ? He knows everything that is in us, and yet He speaks to us with the same unchangeable love and the same unalterable patience as if we were within altogether what we show ourselves without. What a perfect love, then, is this divine and human character of our Master.

4. But if we love Him, we must bear the fruits that are like Him. 'The fruit of the Spirit is charity, joy, peace.'[17] These are the fruit of the Sacred Heart.

[17] Gal. v. 22.

The heart He bears to us we must bear to our neighbour. Our whole mind must be to our neighbour what His mind is to us. And to this we must add a love of the Cross; for that was the crowning perfection of the Sacred Heart. It is not easy to love contradictions, slights, sorrows, anxieties, failures, vexations. We who murmur and repine and chafe and fret all the day long if anything goes against us call ourselves disciples of the Sacred Heart; and yet we have not so much as the will to bear the Cross, much less to love it. We must learn to be forgiving, to be patient, to be severe against the least sin, not in others—we must bear with them in charity, hoping for their salvation—but in ourselves. Be as sharp as you will with yourselves, do not bear with the least sin in your own temper, give no impunity to yourselves or to your own faults. These are the tokens of the true disciples of the Sacred Heart.

I have endeavoured to put before you the dogma of the Sacred Heart in the Sacrament of the Altar; for dogma, as we have seen, generates devotion. One reason why devotion among us is often so low and feeble is because the light of dogma sometimes is not held up in all its peremptory and divine splendour. Truth has a sacramental power of its own.

Wherever truth is lifted up it is the light of a beacon set on high, and the radiance of that light penetrates into the intellect, and through the intellect into the will, and pervades the heart. You that are not members of the Confraternity of the Sacred Heart, lose no time to enrol yourselves. Go to your pastors, and give your names to be entered on the rolls of the confraternity. The obligations are very slight, the benedictions are very great. The obligations are only to say every day one ' Our Father' and one ' Hail, Mary,' and once the baptismal Creed, with this one aspiration, ' O Most Sweet Heart of Jesus, make me to love Thee more and more.' This is the whole obligation. But it puts you into a special and continuous personal relation to the Sacred Heart and to the Divine Person of Jesus ; and being a personal disciple, and in direct personal relation to Him, your whole life will be drawn to His presence. After having enrolled yourselves, I counsel you to consecrate yourselves; that is, to resolve that you will take His Sacred Heart as your model; that you will live according to it ; that you will examine your own heart by it; that you will make it, day by day, the rule of your actions ; that you will come to it as to a fountain. As a thirsty man comes to a fountain of water, so come, day by day, to the Sacred Heart itself, to obtain the grace to be like it : and lastly, make a constant reparation to it for the manifold sins and wrongs and slights that you have committed against it ; and not for your own sins only, but for the sins of all other men.   Live henceforth a life of reparation, endeavouring by your love and by your fidelity to offer, instead of the vinegar and the gall lifted to His lips on Calvary, the consolation and the joy of your generous and grateful service.

Into what sweetness, into what gladness will you enter if you are disciples of the Sacred Heart.   You will understand by experience the words, ' How great is the multitude of Thy sweetness which Thou hast hid for them that fear Thee.'[18] Throughout the whole world, from sunrise to sunset—for in the Kingdom of Jesus the sun never goes down—the Sacred Heart is worshipped day by day.   When the tapers on the altar are lighted for the Holy Mass in our morning, in other regions of the world they are being kindled on the altar for the evening Benediction. And as the sun goes round the world, in the language of men, opening the day, the Holy Mass follows it, and Benediction comes after in its train.   Everywhere Jesus is upon the altar, in the tabernacle, under the canopy of the world-wide Church ; and there are

[18] Ps. xxx. 20.

millions upon millions, and myriads of millions, ador-
ing Him in perpetual worship, and saying, ' Sanctus,
Sanctus, Sanctus ; Holy, Holy, Holy, Lord God of
Sabaoth ; heaven and earth are full of Thy glory.
Hosanna in the highest.'

And that worship upon earth mingles with the
worship of heaven. For before the throne there
are Saints and Martyrs, and Angels and Archangels,
and dominions and principalities and powers, and
virtues and thrones, and Cherubim and Seraphim ;
and in the splendour of eternal glory all created
things are casting their crowns of gold before the
Sacred Heart of Jesus, saying, ' Worship and glory
and thanksgiving and wisdom and praise be unto
Him that sitteth upon the throne.' The Sacred
Heart of Jesus to all eternity will be adored, in the
glory of God the Father

VI.

THE TEMPORAL GLORY OF THE SACRED HEART.

THE TEMPORAL GLORY OF THE SACRED HEART.

His eyes shall see the King in His beauty. Isaias xxxiii. 17.

WHEN the prophet spoke these words, Jerusalem was in fear and desolation. The hosts of Assyria were coming up round about its walls, and the enemy was mighty and confident in his strength. The people of Jerusalem were terror-stricken and conscious of their own weakness. And in that time of anxiety and fear the prophet lifted up his voice, and promised to the inhabitants of Jerusalem that they should yet ' see the King in His beauty ;' that is, the glory of the Son of David, the peace and victory of His Kingdom over all its enemies. But the prophet was gazing on no earthly king when he spoke these words. He was looking upon no created beauty ; the throne of David disappeared in the glory that arose before him ; the walls of Jerusalem passed out of his sight ; it was not Ezechias, it was the Word Incarnate reigning upon His throne, of whose beauty the prophet spoke.

It was the Saviour of Israel, because it was the God of Israel; it was the King of Israel, because it was the Incarnate Son of God. This promise was indeed made to the Jews: but the prophet also says, ' He that walketh in justice . . . and shaketh his hand from bribes, and stoppeth his ears lest they hear blood, and shutteth his eyes that they look not upon evil,'[1] he shall see the King in His beauty. That is to say, no unjust man, no man that worketh iniquity, no man that speaketh falsely, no man that barters truth and justice for bribes, no man that listens to evil, or that looks upon wickedness, shall 'see the King in His beauty.' These words are therefore spoken to every one of us; and the promise and the prophecy shall be fulfilled in us if in the sight of God we be just.

But when and how shall we ' see the King in His beauty'? They saw 'the King in His beauty,' in that midnight when His Blessed and Immaculate Mother laid Him as an infant in the manger at Bethlehem; the shepherds saw Him, and the angels of God worshipped Him. They saw ' the King in His beauty' when the kings from the East came up, bearing their gifts, to lay at the feet of a King greater than themselves. They also saw ' the King in His beauty' who, during the three-and-thirty years of His life

[1] Isaias xxxiii. 15.

while He was visible among men, saw the Son of God Incarnate, of whom the Evangelist writes when he says, ' The Word was made flesh, and dwelt among us; and we beheld His glory, the glory as it were of the Only-begotten of the Father, full of grace and truth.' And we too shall see ' the King in His beauty' if we be pure and just of heart; if we keep a custody over our senses, and guard our soul free from sin, the promise shall hereafter be fulfilled to us, ' The clean in heart shall see God;' we shall see our Lord Jesus Christ, the King of kings and Lord of lords, sitting upon the great white throne, the splendour of which surpasses the noonday sun, in the glory of His Eternal Father. But was this prophecy and this promise only to be fulfilled in the past, or only to be fulfilled in the future? Has it no fulfilment now ? Is not this beauty of the King now visible to our eyes ?   Has it no manifestation except by the light of natural sense as it was in the beginning, or by the light of glory as it shall be hereafter ? The beauty of the King is visible now, manifest at this time.   There is a perpetual manifestation of the beauty of the Word Incarnate; from that hour to this it has never ceased upon earth. There is a vision of faith which is the prelude of the vision of glory. The vision of faith is the vision of the eye and of natural sight taken up into a higher region, according to the words of Jesus Himself when He said, ' Because thou hast seen Me thou hast believed.   Blessed are they that have not seen and yet have believed.'[2]   And therefore now, at this time, to you and to me, this vision of beauty is granted, if we have the light of faith and the eyes of faith to see it.

Let us go on, then, and draw out briefly how this vision of beauty is manifested to us now.

1. First of all, the glory of the Incarnate Word from that hour to this has shone upon the earth, and in that light the beauty of the Eternal Son of God made Man for us is visible to those who believe.   The world was dark, because it had lost the light of the knowledge of God; the world was dark in its intellect, because it had lost the illumination of the knowledge of the true God ; and the world was dark in its heart, because it was dark in its intellect.   Therefore, having lost the knowledge of the true God, it formed to itself hideous and perverted conceptions of many gods, the incorporation of the passions of man; and because its conception of God was perverted and hideous its heart was base, sensual, and depraved.   Such was the state of the old world ; and the prophet describes it when he says, ' Darkness

<hr>

[2] S. John xx. 29.

shall cover the earth, and a mist the people ; but the
Lord shall arise upon thee, and His glory shall be
seen upon thee; and the Gentiles shall walk in thy
light, and kings in the brightness of thy rising.'[3]
This was the first manifestation of the glory of the
Sacred Heart, and its light rose upon the earth in
the star which led the kings from the East, a single
ray of light from heaven in the midnight of the world.
' The Bright and Morning Star'[4] shone in Bethlehem,
and from the lowly roof of the stable it spread its
rays little by little.   In His childhood, in His boyhood, in His youth, in His manhood, in the humble
life which He lived at Nazareth, and in the public
life which He lived in Jerusalem the glory and the
beauty were waxing always brighter.   Then He manifested Himself to His disciples ; and He was manifested as the Son of God in His baptism, when the
Holy Ghost came down, and the voice of the Father
declared Him to be the Son of His good will.   Then
He manifested His glory when He came to dwell in
Galilee, where He wrought His first miracle; He
was manifested in the Transfiguration, where His
countenance ' shone as the sun, and His raiment
became white as snow.'   But these were only the
outward symbols, the visible tokens of a vision of

[3] Isaias lx. 2, 3   [4] Apoc. xxii. 16.

His beauty and His glory, which was for ever growing broader and more luminous in the hearts of
His disciples as the light of faith came down upon
them. Finally, when He rose from the dead, and
in the forty days when He came back to them,
He was manifest in His Godhead and His power,
and the beauty and the glory of the Incarnate
Word were fully revealed. Lastly, the 'Light of
the world' which, as the prophet foretold, arose
as the 'Star out of Jacob,'[5] became as the noonday
sun in its strength, when, on the Day of Pentecost, the illumination of the Holy Ghost was shed
forth as a flood, first upon the Apostles, and then
through them upon the nations of the world. In that
great depth of light the words of the prophet were
fulfilled, that 'the earth is filled with the knowledge
of the Lord, as the covering waters the sea.'[6] The
glory of the Incarnation, shining out from Jerusalem,
has filled the whole world. The Christian world has
light in its dwellings; beyond it the nations lie in
darkness. Wheresoever the Sacred Heart of Jesus
Christ is known, there hangs before the intellect and
the heart of men a vision of beauty; and that vision
of beauty is the vision of God Himself Incarnate,
verifying the words of the Apostle, 'God, who com-

[5] Numbers xxiv. 17.   [6] Isaias xi. 10.

manded the light to shine out of darkness, hath shined in our hearts, to give the light of the knowledge of the glory of God in the face of Jesus Christ.[7] The human countenance of Jesus, radiant with the perfections of the Sacred Heart, is the vision of beauty which has hung for these eighteen hundred years before the intellect and the heart of the Christian world.   No vision of beauty ever surpassed this; none but this has ever manifested the glories of God and the perfections of manhood in one Person.   We see there the beauty of the Divine Person of Jesus Christ, the beauty of His sacred countenance, the beauty of His divine character, and the beauty of His deified human Heart.   It is the beauty of the Incarnate Word, clothed in all the tenderness of our manhood, elevated and glorified in the Person of the Eternal Son.   Here, then, is the first fulfilment; and you, if you be among the just, if you keep custody over your senses, if your heart be clean, have the light of this beauty shining upon you.   If you live lives of prayer and piety and faith, it is as visible before you as the beauty of the world which we see with our eyes of sense.

2. Once more.   This beauty of the heart of Jesus was impressed upon the world.   For it was not only

[7] 2 Cor. iv. 6.

a vision; it was a power. It not only hangs before us as an object of contemplation, but it has a power of transforming all things into its own likeness. The Apostle says, ' We, with open face beholding as in a glass the glory of the Lord, are transformed into the same image from glory to glory, as by the Spirit of the Lord;' that is to say, God has manifested His beauty to the world that He may change the world into its likeness. The first creation which fell from Him by sin fell likewise under the sentence of death; and because it was darkened and defiled, it needed to be regenerated and renewed and created again. The second creation of God is not only perfect, as in the beginning, but is raised to a perfection above its former state. The transfiguration of the world is accomplished by the beauty of the Incarnate Word, that is, by the beauty of the Sacred Heart of Jesus. Wheresoever the light of His knowledge has spread, He has changed the face of the world. He has fulfilled the words of the prophet: ' The land that was desolate and impassable shall be glad; and the wilderness shall rejoice, and flourish as a lily; it shall bud forth and blossom. · The glory of Libanus is given to it; the beauty of Carmel and Saron. They shall see the glory of the Lord and the beauty of our God.'[8] That

<hr>

[8] Isaias xxxv. 1, 2.

is to say, ' the nations that sat in darkness and in the shadow of death' shall first be illuminated; 'they shall see the glory of the Lord and the beauty of our God:' even the very soil under their feet shall bud forth in goodness, and blossom in purity as the lily; the impassable way shall become plain, the path of justice shall be clear as light, men shall walk where before the wilderness was never trodden by foot. The nations of the world, which were as a desert, shall become a garden; from a wilderness they shall be made the paradise of God; that is to say, out of the heathen world shall arise the Christian world; out of the world that was dead in sin shall arise a world of sanctity and life. Such is the one Holy Catholic Church, the mirror of the beauty of the Incarnate Word; holy, because He is holy and the Giver of all holiness; one, because He is the Only-begotten of the Father; universal, because He has shed abroad His light in all the world; imperishable, because He is eternal life. The Kingdom of Jesus Christ has changed the face of the world; wheresoever it has spread it has reclaimed the waste places of the earth, it has subdued them by culture, and has made them to be a field white for the harvest. Such has been the work of the Incarnation. The Sacred Heart of Jesus, which is the love of God clothed in the sympathies of our humanity, has been not only glory and beauty, but an assimilating power, the principle of a new life, changing the inward hearts of men and of nations into the likeness of itself. Every soul born again of the Holy Ghost receives this seed of God. And S. John writes, ‘Whosoever is born of God committeth not sin; for His seed abideth in him, and he cannot sin because he is born of God.’ If any man be in Christ Jesus —and all who are baptised and are born again are in Christ Jesus—‘old things are passed away; and all things are become new.’[9] Wherever the hearts of men have been thus changed, first one by one, then by households, then by villages and towns and cities and peoples and nations, the world has changed its face. It has put off its own likeness, and has put on the image of Jesus Christ. The outward life and the inward Heart of our Divine Redeemer have become the pattern and law to men. And as the world was changed in individuals, households, and kingdoms, the Church of God became the mother and the queen of the nations. They were thereby redeemed from the bondage and corruption of sin into the glorious liberty of the sons of God. In them have been verified the words of Jesus Christ, ‘If the Son shall make you free, you shall be free indeed.’[10] ‘You shall know the truth,

[9] S. John iii. 9. [10] Ibid. viii. 36.

and the truth shall make you free.'[11]   As in the
beginning the serpent tempted man with a false
knowledge to rob him of the truth, so Satan now
tempts men with a false liberty to rob them of the
freedom of the sons of God.   Liberty is not license ;
liberty is not the freedom of madmen ; liberty is not
the power to do wrong, nor to believe falsehood, nor
to err out of the way of justice.   Liberty means
redemption from sin, from falsehood, from human
teachers who may err and therefore can mislead.   It is
redemption from all spiritual tyranny of man over
man, and the liberation of the whole man, with all
his faculties, his intellect, his heart, his will, his affections ; it is a redemption of the soul in all its actions
towards God, in its obedience, in its faith, in its
adoration, by the divine authority of Jesus Christ,
who has purchased us with His Precious Blood,
and has folded us within a unity where falsehood
cannot enter, and under the divine guidance of a
Teacher who can never err.   Such is true liberty,
and there is no other.   The Church of God, then, is
the mother of all true spiritual and religious freedom,
for she it was who taught the nations of the earth
the true domestic, public, civil, and political liberties
of mankind.   There was never liberty before Chris-

[11] S. John viii. 32.

N

tianity; liberty there will never be when Christianity shall cease to guide the government of men.   All true liberty came into the world with Jesus Christ; all true liberty spread from Him among the nations of the world, and with Him true liberty will depart. If men reject the beauty of that King reigning on the throne of truth they will fall under the dominion of falsehood and of force, which will put a yoke of iron on their necks.   The Word Incarnate, who is the second Adam, came and impressed upon the whole race of mankind, so far as they are His disciples, the likeness of Himself.   He has made His own Most Sacred Heart the model and the pattern and the principle by which men may both form their lives and govern the world.   He has stamped a new likeness upon the race of mankind, and that new image is His own, more perfect than the likeness of the first Adam in which we are born, for he was only man; but the second Adam, of whom we are born again, is the Incarnate God.   We are thereby made ‘partakers of the Divine Nature,’[12] and are conformed to the divine perfections.   This also is the vision of ‘the King in His beauty’ by the light of the Sacred Heart.

3. Thirdly and lastly, ‘the King in His beauty’ may be seen in the personal and temporal reign of

[12] 2 S. Peter i. 4.

Jesus Christ in heaven and on earth.   How does He reign on earth temporally and personally ? He reigns by one whom He has appointed to reign in His stead, to speak in His name, and to exercise His supreme jurisdiction.   He has not left Himself without a Vicar.   When He said, ' Thou art Peter, and upon this rock I will build My Church, and the gates of hell shall not prevail against it ;' and when He added, ' and to thee will I give the keys of the kingdom of heaven ; and whatsoever thou shalt bind on earth shall be bound also in heaven, and whatsoever thou shalt loose on earth shall be loosed also in heaven,' He chose out and constituted one who should reign in His stead and fill His own place.   He created also an office which should be perpetual on earth.   He willed that there should for ever be one who should repre-sent Him, one who should feed His sheep, as the Chief Shepherd of the universal flock.   Therefore he is called His Vicar, because he holds the keys and rules by the authority which belongs by right to Himself.   And when He said, ' Behold I am with you all days, even to the consummation of the world,' He promised that the office of His Vicar should never cease.   The world will not believe this.   If men will not believe it, let them account for the fact that there is at this hour a succession of Pontiffs ruling from the See of Peter. Its presence claims a lineal identity. It is here living and reigning; and if the world will not believe it to be unbroken, if it will not believe it to be divine, let it account for its existence and for the obedience of men to its voice. Let the world tell us why the See of Peter has never been destroyed. The world has never ceased to strive against it, and if it had been in the power of man to destroy it, it would have been destroyed long ago. If the world could have wrenched its links asunder they would have long ago been broken. But here it is at this hour. Pius IX. speaks in the name of all the Pontiffs that have ever gone before him—speaks as they ever spoke, full of the living consciousness of a divine commission, in the Name and with the authority of His Divine Master. Here then is 'the King in His beauty,' ' though his visage be inglorious among men, and his form among the sons of men;'[13] 'despised and the most abject of men.'[14] Yet from him alone is derived the jurisdiction to speak to you the words that I am speaking now; and from him alone is received the power to absolve; and the authority to delegate the power of absolution to those who apply to you the pardon of the Most Precious Blood. But I said men will not believe it, and

<hr>

[13] Isaias lii. 14.   [14] Ibid. liii. 3.

they tell us, 'The whole world is rejecting this Vicar of Jesus Christ, as you call him.' I answer, They rejected his Master; and if they rejected the Master, is it any wonder that they reject His Vicar? And did not the Master Himself foretell?—'The disciple is not above the Master, nor the servant above his Lord.' 'If they have called the good man of the house Beelzebub, how much more them of his household.'[15]   It is but a fulfilment of the prophecy, 'You shall be hated of all men for My name's sake.'   If the world loved us, the prophecy would not be fulfilled, and our faith might be shaken; but the prophecy is fulfilled in this, that the world rejects now the Vicar of Jesus Christ, as then it rejected Jesus Christ Himself. Ay, more than this: if there be any head upon earth, sacred and venerable, which is the mark of every stone that every evil or wanton hand can fling, which is pelted every day with all the storms of proud and rebellious tongues, it is the head of the Vicar of Jesus Christ.   The world says to us, 'Look at your Vicar of Jesus Christ: the whole world has not only rejected him and his Temporal Power, but every day in all its tones is telling both him and you what we think of him.' Is it a wonder that the Vicar should not be above his Master? Did they not

15 S. Matt. x. 24, 25.

refuse to believe in Him? Did they not revile Him? Did they not mock Him? Did they not blindfold Him? Did they not say to Him, 'Prophesy who it is that smote thee'? And if they are slighting and mocking His Vicar now it is more than the fulfilment of a prophecy; it is a conformity between the servant and the Master, it is therefore a luminous proof and confirmation of our faith. Once more the whole world is making war against him. 'You tell us,' the world says every day, 'that the nations of the world are Christian, that they are the offspring of the Church of God. Why, these nations have all rejected the Head of your Church; they are making war against him, they are pulling him down on every side.' Why not? They crucified his Master. Is there not here again another fulfilment? Did they not, for three hundred years, crown almost every successive Pontiff with martyrdom? Has not the world, for fifteen hundred years, by subtilty and by force endeavoured to overthrow that sacred throne, and to rob it of the sovereignty which his Divine Master gave to Peter? When the sheep that were appointed for slaughter in the beginning ascended the hill of the Capitol, they, all in one day, found the wolves lying dead upon it. The wolves were dead, and the sheep entered into possession of the inheritance which their

Lord had given them. Nevertheless from that hour to this they have always been the objects of the world's scorn and hatred. Five-and-forty times the Vicars of Jesus Christ have been driven out of Rome, or have never set their foot in it; they have been, from the beginning, martyrs, exiles, fugitives, and prisoners. It has been their common fare, it has been the lot and the inheritance of him who bears the office of the Vicar of the Son of God, who was the first to be mocked, bound, scourged, and crucified; and in this there is revealed the 'beauty of the King,' the beauty of meekness, the beauty of faith, the beauty of inflexibility, the beauty of fearlessness, the beauty of fortitude, and the beauty of fidelity to God and to His truth even unto martyrdom. No man that has the light of faith in him, no man that has a Christian and a manly heart, can surely read the history of the Pontiffs without seeing there a reflection at least of their Divine Master's shame; and this too is the glory of the Sacred Heart.

But Jesus not only reigns personally among men, by an outward sovereignty; He reigns also by an inward sovereignty, by the inflexibility of justice over the will, and by the infallibility of truth over the intellect and the conscience of men—over those that believe, for their joy and their salvation;

over those that will not believe, for their peril and
for their sentence hereafter.   Those who, in bad
faith, lift up their heel against the authority of the
Church of Jesus Christ are condemned of themselves.
Jesus has said, 'For judgment I am come into this
world, that they that see not may see, and they that
see may become blind.[16] If you were blind, you
should not have sin; but now you say, We see.
Your sin remaineth.'[17]

The old world was so full of a belief in God that
it fell into the worship of a multitude of gods.   So far
was atheism from the heart of men in the beginning,
that they invested the visible objects of the world,
even the world itself, with divinity.

The world, which is falling away from the light
of faith, apostatising from Jesus Christ and persecuting His Church, is the world without God, the
atheistical world ; and that atheistical world is the
world that is blind and cannot see the beauty of the
Son of God. It is sinking below the Pantheism of
the pagan world.   It does not believe in Jesus,
therefore it cannot see the impress of God in the
creation of the world.   It does not believe in a
Creator, therefore it cannot read His handwriting.
It sees the sky over its head, and believes in no

[16] S. John ix. 39.   [17] Ibid. 41.

heaven beyond it. It sees the visible horizon, and believes in no mind that governs the universe. It believes in the earth under its feet, because it has had to bury its dead, and it will be buried in the same itself. The material world of this day is without God—is simply atheistic; men live as if they were matter, dust returning unto dust, without belief in the existence of their own souls, or of the immutable distinction of right and wrong, or of judgment to come, or of a state after death. They live without God: they die like the cattle that perish. And if they who die like the cattle live like men, it is a mystery I cannot unravel. The man that lives without belief in God, if he lives a life rational, intellectual, just, pure, and merciful, is a miracle indeed. When faith in God disappears, the soul in man is degraded. In the midst of this world without God, which is enveloped and stifled in matter, the Church is conscious, with a vivid and living consciousness, of an unseen world with which it is vitally united. The Church visible on earth, militant and suffering here, lives by the same life as the Church suffering in Purgatory and triumphant in heaven. We, who believe in the Communion of Saints, are as conscious of that union as they who live in a household are conscious of the existence of all others that are under the same roof.   As the Apostle says, ' You are come to Mount Sion, and to the city of the living God, the heavenly Jerusalem, and to the company of many thousands of angels, and to the Church of the first-born, who are written in the heavens, to the spirits of just men made perfect.'[18]   There is a cloud of witnesses hanging over your heads, you are encompassed by the world unseen; and in the midst of that unseen world there is the heavenly court : there are the nine orders of angels, and the Patriarchs and the Prophets and the Apostles and Martyrs and the Saints and the Confessors surrounding ' the King in His beauty ;' and from that throne He reigns upon earth.   He governs the world by His providence, and He disposes the hearts of men by His Spirit. It is His hand which bears the rod of iron to reign over the nations of the world.   He is bearing with them in patience until the time shall come when He shall bring forth justice unto judgment.

Thus far I have traced out, very imperfectly, the beauty of the King, which is visible now to faith. Therefore to us also the promise is fulfilled.   But though this is visible to faith, it is not visible to those who will not believe.   It is not visible except to those who are clean of heart.   The manifestation of

[18] Heb. xii. 22, 23.

God has never failed, but the eyes of the world have grown dim. 'The light shineth in the darkness, and the darkness did not comprehend it.'[19] He is hid to those ' in whom the god of this world hath blinded the minds of them that believe not, that the light of the Gospel of the glory of Christ, who is the image of God, should shine unto them.'[20]

The Incarnate Word dethroned the world. Its atheism, its idolatries, its corruptions, its cruelties, its immoralities, its philosophies, its superstitions, were all swept away in the light of the Incarnation; but ever since its downfall the world has been striving to dethrone the Incarnate Word. The conflict is going on at this hour; it is now closing in, round about the Church and the Head of the Church, with its last array of power. But it shall not prevail. At this moment, when the world seems to be in its greatest strength, and the Church in its greatest weakness, there never was a time from the beginning when the Church of God was so widespread among the nations of the world—so nearly reaching to its universality; nor was it ever more profoundly united in intellect and heart and will within, nor ever more solid and indissoluble in its unity without. It never manifested at any time to the world the notes of its

[19] S. John i. 5.   [20] 2 Cor. iv. 4.

divine origin and of its divine authority with a broader light, or with a more self-evident witness, than at this day.

Therefore in this time of desolation fear nothing; have confidence in the Sacred Heart, which day by day, in all the Catholic Unity, is known and loved more and more. If the hour of deliverance tarries, it is only because the time is not ripe. Trust in the words of prophecy and of promise: 'His eyes shall see the King in His beauty.' That manifestation will come when the time is come; meanwhile rejoice and be glad. Know that your inheritance is sure, and that you shall enter into its fulness when His will has been accomplished and the number of His elect is gathered in. These dark days are not for ever. The time is at hand when it shall be said to us: 'Thy sun shall go down no more, and thy moon shall not decrease; for the Lord shall be unto thee for an everlasting light, and the days of thy mourning shall be ended.'[21]

[21] Isaias lx. 20.

VII.

THE TRANSFORMING POWER OF THE SACRED HEART.

THE TRANSFORMING POWER OF THE SACRED HEART.

For we all beholding, as with open face, the glory of the Lord, are transformed into the same image, from glory to glory, as by the Spirit of the Lord. 2 Cor. iii. 18.

I HAVE already explained the language of the Church, by which we are taught that the Sacred Humanity assumed by the Son of God is deified. It became the Manhood of God, and, as the Fathers say, it was also deified by the sanctity of God, which pervaded it, as fire pervades the iron in the furnace. In this latter sense the deification of the Sacred Humanity signifies its sanctification.

Now in this latter sense Dionysius (or whosoever be the author of the *Ecclesiastical Hierarchy*), S. Athanasius, S. Cyril, S. John Damascene, and others apply the word to all who are sanctified by union and conformity to Jesus Christ. Dionysius says, ' Deification is an assimilation and union, so far as it can be, with God.'[1] Again, ' The nature of God is the

[1] De Eccl. Hier. cap. i. s. 3.

principle of deification, by which all who shall be deified are deified.'[2]   S. Athanasius says, ' He (the Son of God) assumed our human nature that He might deify us.'[3]   And again, ' He was made man that He might deify us.'[4]

S. John Damascene says that God created man to be deified by approaching to Himself; and he explains the manner of it,—' deified by participation of divine illumination, not changed into the divine essence.'[5]   In this way the Fathers explain the words of the Psalmist quoted by our Lord : ' Ye are gods, ye are all the children of the Most High ;'[6] and again those of S. Peter, ' being made partakers of the divine nature.'[7]   S. Athanasius writes thus against the Arians : ' It is not granted to Him as a reward that He should be called the Son of God; but it is He that has made us to be sons of the Father, and He has deified men, being made man Himself.'[8] Now the meaning of all this is, not that we are made partakers of the divine essence, which is both intrinsically impossible and madness to think, but by adop-

---

[2] Cap. i. s. 4.

[3] Orat. de Incarn. Verbi, tom iv. p. 109.

[4] Ad Adelphium, tom. i. p. 158.

[5] De Fid. Orth. lib. ii. c. xii.

[6] Ps. lxxxi. 6.   [7] 2 Pet. i. 4.

[8] Orat. ii. Contr. Arian. tom. i. p. 345.

tion, by the sanctification of the Holy Ghost, by participation in goodness and illumination, by assimilation, and by conformity.

Therefore conformity to the Sacred Heart of Jesus is our perfection. First, let us see in what that conformity consists; next, the means by which it is wrought in us; and lastly, the signs of it.

What, then, is conformity to the Sacred Heart of Jesus? S. Paul says that 'we all, with open face beholding the glory of the Lord, are transformed into the same image.' And when he says 'we,' he means all Christians, as distinguished from the people of God of old; for he is drawing a contrast between the manifestation of the glory of the Lord in the face of Moses, who, after he had seen God, while his face was shining with the reflection of the divine presence, had need to cover it with a veil, because the people could not endure the splendour of His glory. The Apostle contrasts this with the face of Jesus Christ, which is not only the reflection of God, but the face of God Himself, and this glory we behold without a veil. In the glory of that countenance we see the glory of God with open face. It is manifested and revealed to us; and, so far from needing a veil to intercept that glory, it is by the steadfast contemplation of this glory that the power of transformation works in us. It changes those who gaze upon it 'from glory to glory into the same image.'   In another place S. Paul says, 'God, who commanded the light to shine out of darkness, hath shined in our hearts, to give the light of the knowledge of the glory of God in the face of Jesus Christ.'   Here we have again exactly the same truth, that the face, that is, the human countenance, of Jesus Christ is the manifestation of the glory of God ; and that by gazing on it our hearts are assimilated, and changed by its transforming power into the same likeness.   For as the Apostle says in another place, ' Let that mind be in you which was also in Christ Jesus, who, being in the form of God, counted it not robbery to be equal with God: but, being God Himself, He emptied Himself' (that is, He laid aside His glory), 'and was made in the likeness of man.'[9]   'He took upon Him the form of a servant ;' that is to say, Jesus Christ was in the form of God, because He is God; and He took upon Himself the form of man, being made man— true man, as He is also true God; and that true form of God and true form of man united in one Divine Person constitute the Sacred Heart of Jesus.   There is the eternal charity of God clothed in the sympathies and the affections of man, and in that we see the twofold perfections of the divine and human natures of Jesus Christ. Such, then, is the plain meaning of the text. The face of Jesus Christ signifies the whole Person, in all the perfections, divine and human ; and the manifestation of that perfection is by the Sacred Heart, which is not only a symbol but an organ of the divine and human love of our Redeemer.

And to this pattern all who are saved must be conformed. Salvation is this deification or conformity to the Sacred Heart. No soul which is deformed, that is, which is unlike to the Sacred Heart of Jesus, shall enter the Kingdom of God. No soul can live eternally which is not in union with God. And no soul which is not conformed to the Sacred Heart can be united with God. Therefore conformity to the Sacred Heart is the vital condition of our salvation.

Spiritual writers sometimes put this subject in the following way, in four words—*Deformata reformare, reformata transformare, transformata conformare;* that is, that which is deformed in us must be reformed, that which is reformed must be transformed, and that which is transformed must be conformed to the perfect image of Jesus Christ, who is the form of all perfection, divine and human, being both God and man.

Now there are three kinds of this conformity. There is the transformation of the innocent, and there is the reformation of the penitent, and there is the conformation of the Saints. And all these three, the innocent, the penitent, and the Saints, find the type and the term of their perfection in Jesus Christ.

1. We will begin first with the innocent. And who are they? The innocent are those that are born again and abide in their baptismal grace; the little ones of the Kingdom of God, who never fall from the innocence of their baptism; and those childlike souls who grow up in humility and purity, and to the end of life are childlike as they were in the beginning. Our Lord describes them when He says, 'Unless you be converted and become like little children, you shall in no wise enter into the kingdom of heaven.'[10] Now the most perfect example of this innocence is in the Person of our Lord Himself, in His own childhood, boyhood, youth, and manhood. No shadow could ever fall upon the perfection of divine innocence. Being God, it was impossible in Him. The innocent are those who, being

[10] S. Matt. xviii. 3.

born again by water and the Holy Ghost, are made sons of God, brethren of Jesus Christ; in them the light of faith, if sustained by mental prayer and the contemplation of the Person and the example of our Lord, is always growing; then hope grows into confidence and reliance upon the love and the perpetual care of our Divine Master; and then charity is ever kindling more and more towards God and man, expanding in their hearts, pervading their whole life. In this way they grow up into the likeness of our Lord. They become more and more averted from creatures; and the world, which is the bondage of the soul, has less and less hold over them. They are more and more converted to God by a steady, equable, gradual, uninterrupted, and lifelong change or transformation of their whole mind and heart and will and spirit into the likeness of their Redeemer. They are averted from creatures, because the very essence of sin is this, that the heart of man, which God made for Himself, to be in union with Himself, is turned away or averted from Him and is converted or turned to creatures; so that by all its passions and affections it lays hold of creatures, and loves and serves, that is, worships, them more than God the Creator. But where faith, hope, and charity, and the Spirit of God dwell in the heart and perpetually grow and transform the whole inward life into the likeness of Jesus Christ, the soul loses hold of the creatures one by one; it becomes detached from them, independent of them, and has its happiness in things that are higher than all creation. It is always turning to God: as the moon, which receives continually an increase of the light of the sun, until it is full, so the soul, turning continually towards God, loves God, rests in God, and finds all its good and all its fulness in God.

Now the most perfect example of a heart turned in all its expanse to God was in the Sacred Heart. We are told that Jesus 'advanced in wisdom and age and grace with God and man.'[11] We are not to understand that our Divine Lord grew in grace. His deified soul was full of grace from the first moment of the Incarnation. In Him there was no accession nor augmentation, for it was already full; but there were fuller manifestations, a gradual unfolding in the eyes of men of that which was in Him from the beginning, according to the measures and laws of the humanity which He had assumed. But in S. John, the 'beloved disciple,' who, by a special privilege, was preserved from sin, there was this increase of grace, this continual augmentation

[11] S. Luke ii. 52.

and accession; not only an outward manifestation, but an inward increase of the light and grace of sanctification. In his innocence he grew up: as the morning light from the day-spring continually grows to the noontide, or as the ripening of the harvests and of the fruits of the earth, which, with a silent onward progress, continually advance to their full maturity, so it was, without interruption and without break, in the life of the disciple whom Jesus loved.

You will say, perhaps, that there is no such innocence as this now. Yes; your little children are such: they are still in a state of innocence. Watch over and guard them well. If you do this, they may not, indeed, be like the beloved disciple, because they have no such special privilege of grace as he had, but still they may abide in their innocence without mortal sin to their lives' end. God, on His part, will give them all graces necessary for holy perseverance; and they will be perpetually transforming and transformed into the image of Jesus Christ; that is, the Holy Ghost, by whom they were born again, will perpetually accomplish His own work in them. This, then, is the first example of conformity to the Sacred Heart of Jesus.

2. Now the second is, at first sight, more difficult to understand. How, and in what manner, can it be said that the penitent is conformed to the Sacred Heart of our Lord? How can it be said that the sinful is conformed to the Sinless? First of all, our Divine Saviour was made sin for us, though He knew no sin. He stood in the place of sinners; His Heavenly Father dealt with Him as a sinner for the sake of sinners. He laid on Him the iniquity of us all, and 'by His stripes we are all healed.' He suffered for sin all His life. From the first moment of the Incarnation began the oblation of Himself for sin; He was the Man of Sorrows from the first instant that He took our manhood. From the first moment that the human soul was assumed and deified in the Person of the Son of God, He was conscious of the sins of the world and of the sorrow which is inseparable from that sin, because He made Himself the offering for sin. And for three-and-thirty years He was the Man of Sorrows; He bore for us the mental sorrow we ought to bear for our sins. For three-and-thirty years He offered Himself by a willing and continuous expiation. His sinless humanity endured, I may say, the penance of our sins. He bore temptations and hunger, thirst and weariness, fasting and sleepless

nights, scourging and buffeting; He was crowned with thorns; He was nailed upon the Cross. No life of penance ever went beyond the sufferings of the innocent Son of God. He was tempted like to us in all things, sin only excepted;[12] and yet He was made like to us in respect to sin in all its sorrows, except only its guilt; He had all the innocent infirmities of our nature, and all the penalties which follow upon our sin, except those which imply the guilt of the person: He suffered, He tasted them all; and with a sensitive capacity of sorrow which none but the Sinless can know, and a Divine Sanctity alone can suffer.

Therefore the Sacred Heart of Jesus, in its passion upon earth, its three-and-thirty years of perpetual sorrow of mind, its agony in the garden, its anguish upon Calvary, and in all its unknown sufferings, is the example of the penitent. What does it teach us? First of all, that they who are entangled in creatures and averse from God are thereby deformed, destroyed, and dead; and that there is no way of return to God but by the mortification of the passions, affections, and senses whereby we lay hold of creatures, and creatures lay hold of us. Next, that there is no way of life for

[12] Heb. iv. 15.

those that are sinful but union with God, returning to God, conversion to God: that the very intellect becomes darkened, deformed, perverted; the heart becomes corrupt, sensual, and selfish; the will becomes unstable and stubborn; the whole inward nature of man is destroyed by conversion to creatures and aversion from God. We must come back again by conformity to that perfect image of innocence suffering for sin. We must put off not only the practice of sin, the wilful commission of sin, but also the love of sin, and the disorders, affections, and senses of sin. We must mortify them and die to them, and we must return to God and live in and for God above all. Hear the words of the Apostle: 'They that are Christ's have crucified their flesh with the vices and concupiscences.'[13] They must drive the nails through their evil passions. You know, each one, what yours are : every man has his own, every woman has her own. Learn what they are; know them for yourselves, and drive the iron through that affection or that passion which deforms your soul. When you are dead to it, so far you will be conformed to the Sacred Heart of Jesus. Once more the Apostle says, 'With Christ I am nailed to the Cross.'[14] He says 'I;' not one passion or one

13 Gal. v. 24.   14 Ibid. ii. 19.

affection only, but 'I,' that is, my whole soul is stretched out, as it were, nailed hands and feet, and my side is pierced upon the Cross with Christ—'I am nailed to the Cross, nevertheless I live, yet not I, but Christ liveth in me; and the life that I now live in the flesh I live by faith in the Son of God, who loved me and delivered Himself for me;'[15] that is, gave Himself over to die for me. And then, once more, S. Paul says, 'God forbid that I should glory save in the Cross of our Lord Jesus Christ, by whom the world is crucified unto me, and I unto the world.'[16] If these words were not the words of the Holy Ghost, written in Holy Scripture, I should not have dared to speak them. They are divine truth. Unless the sinner dies to sin, dies to the world, and dies to self, he will never enter into the Kingdom of God; unless by mortification all that is deformed is crucified and dead, and by sanctification his whole soul in all its affections, powers, and faculties is conformed to the Sacred Heart of Jesus, he can never be united to God in eternity. Let us take two examples. Take, first, the example of S. Mary Magdalen. Who departed further from the sanctity of the Sacred Heart than she? And yet who ever stood nearer to the Cross? and who ever, with a

<hr>

[15] Gal. ii. 20.   [16] Ibid. vi. 14.

divine indignation, infused into her soul by the Holy Ghost, so chastised and expiated the sins that she had committed? She was conformed to the Sacred Heart of her Master, by detestation of the sins which had stained her, and by love to the Redeemer who had saved her from eternal death. Or, once more, take S. Paul, who was accomplice to the murder of S. Stephen, and whose whole life was spent in a burning zeal of penance, like the zeal for the house of God which consumed his Lord. Here we see, then, that the penitent must be conformed to the Sacred Heart of our Divine Redeemer in these things: sorrow for sin, hatred of all evil, self-denial, self-sacrifice, and crucifixion of his own will. But penance is a hard word; and be sure of what I say, any man who sets about this work, either trusting in his own strength or only by human rules, will never do it. But there is a way of accomplishing it which is both easy and sweet, and I will tell you what it is: it is to sit humbly at the feet of our Divine Lord in the Most Holy Sacrament, to look up into His face, on which there is no veil, into that face which reflects the love and the grace and the tenderness and the absolution and the pity of God Himself, and to gaze upon that countenance until the Spirit of the Lord has transformed you by inward submission into the purity and the sorrow and self-chastisement of your Divine Redeemer.

3. And then, thirdly, there is the conformation of the Saints. But of this I hardly know what to say. Neither you nor I are Saints, nor, in this world perhaps, ever will be. And yet some of you may be. There may be some poor humble soul who hears me who thinks that he is the worst of sinners; there may be some poor woman who says that 'no soul was ever farther from being a Saint than I am;' and yet it may be that those two are nearer than we are in their conformity to the humility of Jesus, for 'the last shall be first and the first last.' But of one thing I am sure—that if there be such they will be the least conscious of it; and if anybody here thinks well of himself, and that he is in the way to be a Saint, he is very far—perhaps the farthest—from it. Our Divine Lord is the King of Saints. He is the elder Brother of Saints, and His humility is the family likeness, the one type, which is common to all His brethren. It is universal in the whole Communion of Saints; for as the light of heaven is one—and yet 'one is the glory of the sun, another the glory of the moon, and another the glory of the stars, for star differeth from star in glory;'[17]

[17] 1 Cor. xv. 41.

and more than this, as each star has its own magnitude and its own colour—for there are coloured rays which diversify the light of every star—so it is with the Saints. All are like to their Divine Master in lowliness, and all are conformed to the Sacred Heart; but no two are identical; yet in this they all agree—they all have a due aversion from creatures, and they all are converted with their whole soul to God. I do not say in this world, but before the Throne to them God is all in all. And when I say they have an aversion from creatures, do not misunderstand me, as if the love of God extinguishes the love of man. No; the love of our neighbour springs from the love of God; the love of kindred, the love of friends, the love of all that are about us is a part of the love of God. As radiance is a part of light, so the love of mankind flows in a direct stream from the love of God. Therefore aversion from creatures means this, that there are no undue attachments, no dependencies, no bondage to creatures, even to the purest and the best. The soul is in perfect liberty because it is united with God; it loves every one, each in his measure, and fulfils every duty of charity with a delicate tenderness greater by far than the love of those who love God less. In the measure in which we love God, in that measure we shall have more heartfelt love to all that are about us. A father will be a better father, and a mother a better mother; son and daughter will be better children; they will love each other more, and friends will love one another more in the measure in which they love God more. Therefore aversion from creatures means a rational and measured love which sets us free from all undue attachments. Then, next, Saints have often said that they had two conversions; their first conversion was from sin to penance, their second conversion was from penance to perfection; that is to say, they began by putting off and mortifying everything they knew to be contrary to the will of God and to the example of the Sacred Heart of our Lord; and having done penance, and chastised themselves for the past, then they went beyond this. To keep the commandments of God is an absolute necessity for salvation; but after we have kept the letter of the commandments, there is the spirit of each commandment, and there are the counsels of liberty and generosity, which any one who desires to serve God with his whole heart will certainly fulfil. If a man gives an alms in some small, if it be not a niggard, measure, he is fulfilling a Christian's duty; his conscience need not reproach him. But if a man were to say to himself, ' I will give a tithe of all I. possess,' or 'I will give a third of all that I gain,' or 'I will give a half of my inheritance,' he is plainly going beyond the measure of necessity : it is an act of generosity. Or, again, if any one were to say, 'I know it is lawful for me to enjoy innocent pleasures; but the money that I might spend on innocent pleasures I will lay by and give to the poor' —there is no strict necessity for doing this ; but in doing it we are moved by a greater generosity. And this is the meaning of S. James when he says, ' So speak ye and so do as being to be judged by the law of liberty ;'[18] that is, 'You were free to do it, and you were free not to do it, but you did it for My sake. I knew every act of self-denial; I knew everything that you laid aside ; I knew everything in which you denied yourself; I knew every motive of every act : you did it for the love of Me.' This is the spirit of counsel, which guides us and lifts us to higher and more perfect actions.

Now I will try to give you a rule by which you may conform yourselves to the Sacred Heart of our Divine Lord. Religious orders, as you know, have a rule and constitutions. I will give you a rule and constitutions for those who live in the world ; and if you will make them your meditation, you will grow

[18] S. James ii. 12.

in conformity and be transformed into the image of the Lawgiver from whom alone they come. Now the rule I will give you is this: 'Thou shalt love the Lord thy God with thy whole heart, with thy whole soul, with thy whole mind, and with thy whole strength; and thy neighbour as thyself.' I did not make that rule: you know who made it. He gave it to all men, and, alas, few men keep it. Now make a resolution with yourselves, in honour of the Sacred Heart, that you will endeavour to keep this rule of perfection. Take that rule as your rule of life.

Next, you will need constitutions, that is to say, explanations, or amplifications of the rule reduced to detail. I will give you two chapters. The first chapter is the Twelve Fruits of the Holy Ghost. Meditate upon them one by one, and try to transcribe them into your own lives. And the other chapter is the Eight Beatitudes. Endeavour to attain them: 'Blessed are the poor in spirit; blessed are the meek; blessed are they that mourn; blessed are they that hunger and thirst after justice; blessed are the merciful; blessed are the clean in heart; blessed are the peacemakers; blessed are ye when men shall persecute you for justice' sake.' There you will find the surest rule of conformity to the Sacred Heart of our Lord; and to those who keep it there will be three chief results. The first is, you will be humble; the second is, you will be charitable; and the third is, you will love the Cross. In all that crucifies your will and crosses your heart's desire; in all that against which other men chafe and fret, and over which they lose their self-control, you, when it befalls you, will say to yourselves, 'This is the discipline of perfection; this is the sign that the Spirit of the Lord is transforming me into the image into which I desire to be changed. I will gladly live and die under this cross, if only I can be made like to the Sacred Heart of Jesus.'

Now I have touched on these three kinds of conversion most imperfectly, as I am well aware; but you will see that in all these three—the innocent, the penitent, and the Saints—the Sacred Heart is the pattern, that the process of transformation is continuous, and that the power whereby that transformation is effected is our co-operation with the Holy Ghost working in us.

As I said before, we are not Saints. No; but we are, I hope, in the way to the kingdom of Saints, and to the throne of the great King of Saints; and as the first rays of the daybreak are the same in kind as the splendour of the noonday sun, I hope our faint beginnings will one day be made perfect, either here or in Purgatory. But do not imagine that the work is done yet. I do not think that anybody is likely to fall into so great an error. All our conformity to the Sacred Heart is the work of God in us; and He perfects it in measure and degree as He sees to be for our good. He humbles us by making us wait. We desire to be sanctified with great speed, that we may be delivered from the bondage of our temptations. We pray to be Saints out of love to ourselves; and if we were made Saints to-day, we might fall to-morrow, as the angels did, by self-contemplation. No; God will make us perfect as He sees fit; every holy thought is from Him, every good desire, every beginning of better things. We should never turn towards Him by a hair's-breadth if He did not first give the attraction and the impulse. His grace prevents us in everything. As the good shepherd goes out after the lost sheep, and the lost sheep would never find its way home if the good shepherd did not first go out to seek it, so the Holy Spirit of God searches for us, and begins to turn us to Himself; and having begun that work in us, He carries it on and gives His grace in measure and in season, according to the needs and dangers of every soul. In Baptism we received a sacramental grace to make us children of God, and to enable us

to fulfil all the duties of a child of God; and there
is no duty, no obligation upon a child of God that a
baptised soul, in its baptismal grace, has not the
power and strength to fulfil. In our Confirmation
we received the grace to be good soldiers of Jesus
Christ—a measured grace proportioned and sufficient
for every conflict. In our Communions we receive a
grace straight from the Sacred Heart, to transform
us into its likeness. If the many Communions that
we have made from the day of our First Communion
had been worthily made, we should now be disciples
of the Sacred Heart indeed. You have been for ten,
twenty, forty years in the practice of Communion,
and I know not how often—and one Communion has
in it grace enough to make us Saints—and what are
you after all? We are straitened not in Him but in
ourselves. In every Communion we receive grace
enough to conform us to the Sacred Heart; and if we
fail in conformity to His perfection, it is because we
on our side have hearts narrow and cold. Nevertheless He bears with us in patience, and holds us fast
with His love. What He begins, if we do not destroy
it, He will perfect through our whole life. This process of transformation is His own, supernatural and
divine—the operation of the uncreated Spirit of God.
He it is who is working now in every one of you; and

therefore 'with fear and trembling work out your salvation,' for this divine reason, that it is 'God that worketh in you to will and to accomplish.'[19]   What is good in you is from Him.   But it is not only His work—it must be yours too.   Throughout the whole process of your salvation, with the exception of the first grace of all, your will must be united with His —you must work together with Him.   We have the power at any moment to cast ourselves into eternal death; we have the power at any moment to commit spiritual self-murder; we may abuse our freedom and commit mortal sin at any time.   God will indeed by His grace draw and resist and warn us; but He will not overbear our free will.   He created that free will to His own image, and He respects the work of His own hands.   He will not deface His own image in us.   But we may also co-operate with Him in every gift of His grace, because He never commands anything that is impossible.   Therefore whosoever will use faithfully the grace that he has received shall receive greater grace; and whosoever asks for more shall surely receive it.

May God in His mercy perfect that work in you. You know the restless activity of your intellect.   Is it conformed to the intelligence of Jesus by the

[19] Philip. ii. 13.

knowledge of the perfect truth which He has re-vealed? Are you illuminated with the faith which He has declared for our salvation? Or are you seeking for it? Or are you doing what tens of thousands are doing now, with a reckless scepticism explaining it away, and, as it were, filing asunder the links of truth which God has laid open to the reason of man to be known and believed upon His divine authority? Next, you are conscious of the turbulence of your heart. Is it yet detached from the world? Is it united in love with our Divine Redeemer? And you know the instability and the impetuosity of your will. Is your will submissive to His will? Are you docile to His divine inspirations? Are you ready to obey His divine voice, to believe what He teaches, to do what He commands?

I have said that we are not yet Saints. But we are all called to be Saints—if not here, at least here-after. And there is one thing we are all called to be, from which no man can release himself. The obligation is universal upon every man to be conformed to the example of Jesus Christ, and the example of Jesus Christ is not the example of His outward life alone. We are not called to be whited walls; we are called also to the inward perfection of His Sacred Heart. He Himself has said it, and His words shall be my last: 'Take up My yoke upon you, and learn of Me; for I am meek and lowly of heart.' Answer to Him and say, 'Lord, make my heart to be like Thy Heart.'

VIII.

THE SURE WAY OF LIKENESS TO THE SACRED HEART.

THE SURE WAY OF LIKENESS TO THE SACRED HEART.

Take up My yoke upon you, and learn of Me; for I am meek and lowly of heart, and you shall find rest for your souls. S. MATT. xi. 29.

I HAVE spoken of the conformity which all must attain to the Sacred Heart of our Lord Jesus Christ. To be united with God we must be conformed to the image of His Son; for if we be not conformed to the image of His Son, united with God we cannot be; and if we be not united with God, we cannot be saved. This was our last subject. I then pointed out,—from the words of S. Paul, where he says, 'We all, beholding, as with open face, the glory of the Lord, are transformed into the same image, from glory to glory, as by the Spirit of the Lord,'[1]— that through the whole of our life, from our earliest consciousness to our latest moments, there must be a perpetual change—a transformation, always advancing, from the great deformity in which all are born

[1] 2 Cor. iii. 18.

to perfect and final conformity to the likeness of Jesus Christ. We saw also that, for those who have fallen from their baptismal innocence, the transformation must begin in a reformation, that what has been defaced and destroyed must be begun over again. It must be reformed, and this does not only signify corrected, but the form which they had before must be reproduced in the soul; and lastly, that those who are reformed must be conformed to the mind of Christ, and that conformation signifies the full and perfect likeness, so far as we can attain it in this world, to the perfection of our Divine Lord.

We have now to consider the means whereby we may attain that full conformity. Those means are twofold: they are either on God's part, or they are on our part. On God's part they are, first, the revelation of His glory, as S. Paul calls it; that is to say, the image of God in the Face of Jesus Christ, or the full perfection of sanctity, of purity, of truth, and of humility, strange as the word may seem, for by the Incarnation God has assumed even lowliness into His perfections. Again, God perfects His servants, first, by the sanctifying grace of His Holy Spirit; secondly, by His holy Sacraments; thirdly, by the discipline of His Providence; and lastly, by the crosses and chastisements which He lays upon them, and by these means He conforms them to the image of His Son.

But it is not my purpose to speak of the means which God employs on His part; my purpose is to speak of the means on our part, that is to say, of what we must do--of that which is within our power, and therefore within our duty.

1. Now, first of all, those who are baptised have been planted in grace, and that from their infancy. If they retain their baptismal innocence and persevere steadfastly in the sanctifying grace which they have received in their regeneration, they may from that hour perpetually grow into a closer and closer conformity to the likeness of the Sacred Heart of Jesus. The first condition, then, on our part is this : a constant fidelity to the grace of our Baptism. You are perhaps conscious, in looking back on your past life, of whole tracts and periods since your earliest consciousness, in which you have failed to correspond with your baptismal grace. Some of you, perhaps, remember how you have broken away from it altogether, how you have cast behind you the law of God, and grieved the Spirit of God, and have departed from the way of holiness; others, again, who, by God's mercy, have been restrained from so great a fall, nevertheless are conscious how, from their earliest

childhood, they have been grieving the Holy Spirit of God by a multitude of petty faults, constantly growing in number and, it may be, in deliberation—how faults have multiplied over their whole character, and, though they have never come to any great downfall such as the world can know, and therefore have not, perhaps, altogether forfeited their baptismal grace, nevertheless they have retarded the continual expansion of the spiritual life which was planted in them in their regeneration. We read in the Lives of the Saints that many of them—I might almost say most of them; for perhaps I should not err far from the truth if I were to say that, as a rule, those who have become conspicuous among the Saints of the Church—have had mothers of great holiness of life, and that their early training has preserved them in the grace of their Baptism. I will take, for example, S. Anselm, the Archbishop of Canterbury, of whom we read that his mother was a Saint, and that she taught him from his earliest infancy to know his Heavenly Father. There is recorded in his life a beautiful example of the childlike conception he had of God. He dreamed one night that he was high up in the Alps over his native place, and that he was in the midst of a great reaping-field; and in the midst of the reaping-field he saw the Lord of

the harvest. The master of that field called him
to come. Anselm came to him with the confidence
of a child, conscious at the same time that he was in
the Divine Presence; and the Lord of the harvest
asked him his name. He told him, with the simplicity of a child, that his name was Anselm. The
Lord of the harvest gave him his blessing and a piece
of white bread. Now, I ask you, whence came that
train of images? How could a child, in his sleep,
have such a vision of truth and beauty? You will not
say it was inspired. Then, if it was not inspired, it
was learnt; and if it was learnt, from whom? A
holy mother; and the continual instruction which fell
from her lips had made the thought of God as a
Father, and this intimate and personal relation of
love a familiar thought to her child. Therefore, in
his dream he had no fear of approaching his Heavenly
Master, and when asked his name he told it with
simplicity and confidence. Now I give this only as
an illustration—I am not using it as an argument
for anything, but as an example—to show what a
holy mother may do with a child that is 'born
again;' how, when the Spirit of God is in the
soul of a child, a watchful and holy mother can train
up an innocent soul from his infancy in a familiar
and confiding knowledge of God. I might also take

the example of S. Edmund of Canterbury, whose mother was eminent for holiness. She also, from his earliest years, taught him in like manner to know God. The whole of his boyhood and youth is full of all manner of tokens that his first thought of God was the love of God.

They who are in their baptismal innocence have a special affinity with the Divine Justice; they walk before God without fear, because in them there is no malice; and the presence of God has no terror, for they think of Him, not so much as a judge, but as a father. They are ignorant of evil; they have not yet learnt that which the men and women of the world believe to be the perfection of a manly or a mature character, that is, familiarity with the evil of this world, which cannot be known without a loss of unconsciousness of evil. To be ignorant of the evil of the world is a grace; to be familiar with its evil is a temptation and a soil. Children who are innocent and ignorant of evil have a special affinity with the Kingdom of God and with the Spirit of God and with the mind of God. They understand things which those who believe themselves to be cultured intelligences cannot comprehend. When S. Paul says that Christ crucified was to the self-trusting Jews a stumbling-block and to the cultured Greeks foolishness, he expresses this same truth. There is between the minds of little children and the mysteries of revelation a kindred and a sympathy, so that they receive them as by intuition, and understand them better than their teachers. The Psalmist says, 'I was wiser than my teachers because I kept Thy commandments.' The mind of a little child is larger and more expanded for the conception of revealed truth than the mind of philosophers and sceptics, who narrow their understandings with unreasonable and pertinacious doubt. And in such innocent and unconscious souls there is a perpetual growth of the spiritual life, a continual formation, an accretion, as we see in the forest tree, which, year by year, puts out an additional ring in the solidity of its stem ; and in its bulk and stature is continually though insensibly growing. So it is in the spiritual life of those who are faithful to their baptismal grace. In truth, little children are the nearest to the Saints ; and those who have childlike minds are the most saintly. Our Divine Lord has, twice over, taught us this. He said, ' Unless you be converted, and become as little children, you shall not enter into the kingdom of heaven ;'[2] and again He said, ' I confess to Thee, O Father, Lord of heaven and earth'—that is, I thank Thee,—'because

[2] S. Matt. xviii. 3.

Thou hast hid these things from the wise and prudent'—in their own eyes—' and hast revealed them unto little ones : yea, Father; for so it hath seemed good in Thy sight.'[3] And therefore the first and chief means of our conformation is that we should be faithful with an even and continuous fidelity to our baptismal grace.

2. And the second means is that we should make good confessions. Now why does the world hate the confessional ? I will tell you in a word. Because the men of the world are afraid of laying their heart open. They know that there are black spots, that there are dark stains, deep wounds, old scars, open sores, and they hide them in darkness. The innocent have no fear, for their hearts are unspotted; and though conscious of many faults and many weaknesses, they are free from the stains and the wounds of an evil life. They are not afraid : to them confession is easy. But those who are conscious that they are carrying within them a secret which the world does not know, of which their neighbours are not aware, which the nearest to them does not suspect, which they would rather die than reveal— according to the shrinking of flesh and blood, forgetting all the while that God knows everything—

[3] S. Matt. xi. 25, 26.

they fear and hate the thought of confession. This is the true reason why the world rails against confession; this is the reason why every revolution that breaks out at once burns the confessional. It dare not come near the confessional. When it sees a confessional it sees a forerunning witness of the Great White Throne and of the Day of Judgment; and to get rid of this intolerable reality the antichristian revolution tears it out from the church and burns it in the streets. They who have kept their baptismal grace have no fear of the confessional. Why should they? What have they got to say? A great many omissions, a great many infirmities, a great many faults, and a great many temptations, it may be, but no habits of indulged sin; there are no stains of deliberate acts, none of those deep and searing recollections of an evil life. Therefore they come readily; and like children, as they spiritually are, they say at once, kneeling under the crucifix in the confessional, so far as they know, all that their Heavenly Father has against them. It is because men break God's law in their hearts that they fear to confess. Therefore they put off their confession until it becomes hard; for if they put it off, they begin to be careless, and they lay up new matter, and that matter multiplies, and the longer they put it off the more unwilling they grow. But those who are still in their baptismal innocence go on continually from light to light; they go on knowing themselves more and more perfectly every time they come to confession, bringing with them no necessary matter of absolution, because no mortal sin; they bring with them, indeed, many a venial sin, which does not break their friendship with God, for such sins come from infirmity and not from deliberation, or, at least, not from malice. And they are pardoned freely by the Precious Blood of our Divine Lord in their perfect absolution. You will find, therefore, that all those who are faithful to the grace which is in them love the Sacrament of Penance. Here is the difference between those whose conscience does not accuse them, and those whose conscience gives them a rebuke: the former come freely and gladly to accuse themselves, and the latter shrink away. The second way, then, to maintain this state of innocence before God is the habit of frequent and good confession.

3. The third way is to avoid the occasions of sin. We must therefore understand exactly what the occasions of sin are. The Tempter covers the whole face of the earth with all manner of snares. He spreads his nets in every path of life. The world, too,

covers itself over with toils. There are temptations of various kinds, in all manner of unlawful, forbidden, and evil things. But these are not the occasions of sin of which I speak. Every temptation, indeed, is an occasion of sin; but the occasions of sin of which I am speaking are not always temptations to things that are evil. An innocent conscience will at once start back from such temptations. An innocent person, who lives in the fear of God, having the spirit of piety in him, if he be tempted to any action visibly and sensibly evil, would be shocked and start aside. The Tempter often defeats himself, and temptations become warnings to awaken the conscience; but an occasion of sin means something which is lawful, innocent, and harmless in itself, but nevertheless may, by some circumstance, either in others or in ourselves, be an occasion of falling. Let me take an example. It is lawful for us to use food and drink; and yet food may be the occasion of delicacy, indulgence, pampering of the body, and thus may be made the occasion of gluttony; and gluttony is one of the seven capital sins. Drink also is lawful, but drink may be intoxicating. Like poison, it may be lawfully taken, but not in a measure to destroy life or reason or moral sense. It becomes unlawful if the measure of it be unlawful. No man may take poison and destroy his life, and no man may take intoxicating drink and destroy his brain. He may take poison to allay pain, and he may take intoxicating drink if he believes that it sustains his strength. Many physicians do not believe it, but others do; and while physicians debate, men will choose what they like best. But if a man abuses it, I say more, if women abuse it—if the refined, from want of watchfulness over their habits, from an indulgence of their palate, or for the purpose of stimulating a languid and wearied frame, worn out by the excitements of society, or to keep up the flagging animal spirits after long hours of senseless talk and depressing waste of life; if they form the secret habit of taking wine and intoxicating drink unknown to any one but God—and this stealthy habit is formed, I am sorry to say, every day by the refined and the delicate, whom the world never suspects—then this fatal abuse may become a bondage from which they may never be freed, and in which at last, in a miserable unconsciousness, they die. Do not think that I am saying these things for the mere purpose of rhetorical effect. I have seen these wrecks, I have stood by them, I have watched them as they have settled down. I have seen strong drink mastering the conscience and the will as the sea encroaches on the shore, until there was no help and no hope left. This is what I call an occasion of sin—a lawful thing abused. I might take many other examples. I will only take one more: I mean friendships. Nothing can be more lawful, nothing can be more innocent, nothing can be more helpful, if the friendship be good: nothing can be more dangerous, nothing more insidious, nothing more corrupting, if the friendship be evil. A bad book is a great evil, but a bad friend is worse. The whisper of a bad friend at the ear of an unwary soul is the most dangerous of all occasions. Friendship has a power of assimilation. A bad friend will change you into his own likeness. I say, then, that the avoiding the occasion of sin, watchfulness over what we do, where we go, what habits we form, what friendships we make, in what measure we indulge ourselves in the things that are lawful—is one of the surest means of conformity to the Sacred Heart.

And here let me say one word to fathers and mothers. You are not conscious of the harm that you do, or allow to be done, to your children, by taking them into the midst of pleasures, the very sounds and sights of which you know to have a taint upon them. You say that you believe your children are too young to be hurt. Believe it not. Sometimes a silent child sits in the midst of grown people, while their tongues are going, without bridle or caution, of matters which they think the child cannot understand; but that young intelligence drinks-in every word; and though the conceptions formed may not be of the same experienced accuracy as in those who speak, they are abundantly sufficient to sow the seeds of evil in the soul, to awaken dangerous curiosities which taint it, and come out fatally some day in after life. I have sometimes listened in amazement at the unguarded license of speech, the surpassing imprudence, with which grown people will speak in the presence of the young. Those young ears are quick to hear, and those young hearts are quick to understand, beyond all that you can conceive. There is an old saying, even of the heathen, that 'great reverence is due to a boy.' The actions, the examples, the words, the conduct of grown people in the presence even of little children, ought to be under a great restraint. You will remember the words of our Lord: Woe to him that shall cause to offend one of these little ones. 'It were better for him that a millstone were tied about his neck, and that he were cast into the sea.'[4] And again He said, 'Their angels in heaven always see the

[4] S. Matt. xviii. 6.

face of My Father who is in heaven.'[5] These silent children have guardian angels, who are looking up into the face of God, and looking down in wonder upon you if, through your imprudence, you either act or speak unwisely in their presence.   And once more. I have no doubt the fathers and mothers who hear me have had among their children some one whom they have thought precocious; and it is a common saying, 'Such a child, I believe, will not be long in this world; he seems not fit for it; he is always talking of God; he has always in his mouth the name of our Lord; he seems to have a sort of affinity to things of the world to come; he is not long for this life.' Now do you believe that this early ripeness is something morbid or exceptional? Not at all. It is the state in which all baptised children might be, if you were faithful and watchful in training them for God. I do not say every baptised child would be in this state, but I say might be. I cannot doubt that you yourselves have known what you would call examples of early piety, of habitual consciousness of the Divine Presence, of ardent love for holy things, of vivid perception of the love and the Passion of our Divine Lord—of heartfelt sympathy with everything that relates to His Person—far

[5] S. Matt. xviii. 10.

beyond all you have in yourselves. What does it come from? It comes from the grace of their Baptism, which continually expands within them, if only the scenes that are round about them, the atmosphere of their homes, the influence of your lives, the occasions of sin, shall not taint or suppress the growth of their spiritual life.

4. Another means of this conformity is the knowledge of ourselves. Why is it that so few people have a thorough knowledge of their own character? I believe it is this: they have not steadily grown up in the light of the Divine Presence; they have gone out from it, at certain periods of their life, into the outer darkness; and when they have returned into the light again, they are like men that come into a light too great for their sight to bear; they have lived for a time unconscious of their own state, and they have not been able to catch up again the threads, and to keep pace with the growth of their own natural character. From this it comes that they understand other people better than they understand themselves; and they have in them a self-love which always dims their view of themselves. Our own hearts are deceitful; there is nothing more difficult to unravel, and therefore self-knowledge is a rare thing. There are three lights in which we can always know ourselves if we will.

The first is the light of God's presence. If we would only place ourselves every day in the presence of the divine perfections; if we would make a meditation of a few moments upon the infinite sanctity of God, the infinite purity, the infinite truth, the infinite justice, and the infinite mercy of God, and then compare ourselves with these perfections : 'Am I holy, am I pure, am I truthful, am I just, am I charitable, am I compassionate, after the example of my Divine Master? Alas, I know this, that "His eyes are as a flame of fire ;" and when He looks into me, He sees how deformed and how unlike to Him I am. I know that in His sight the moon shineth not, and the stars are not pure ; and what, then, am I ?' If we only placed ourselves in this light every day, and often in the day, we should begin to know ourselves.

But there is another light in which to see ourselves—the light of the Sacrament of Penance. Whenever a man makes a true and good confession, he acquires more inward light to know himself; it is a part of the sacramental grace which is given with absolution. We read in the history of the Church of great Saints who went to confession every day of their lives, for instance, S. Charles, the great pastor and Archbishop of Milan. You might ask, What could he have to say? what could he find of which to accuse himself? He lived a holy life in perpetual self-denial, giving himself altogether for his flock,—what could he have to confess? He had, indeed, no mortal sins to confess,—no; nor had he many venial sins. Perhaps not. But he may have had many omissions and temptations, many interior movements of impatience, of resentment, of a strong will, ready to battle with all that came across its path. Because he was a Saint he had a consciousness of internal imperfections, of a warfare and a tumult within him which we have still more, but do not perceive. You do not think these things matters of confession; but he did. He compared himself with the perfections of his Master; and if we did so, we should see that the things which we condone and absolve in ourselves so readily are of the nature of sin. Next, perhaps, he never lay down at night without being conscious of a great many omissions throughout the day, of good left undone, of opportunities which he had not used, of occasions in which he might have given help to some soul, or have spoken a word that might have brought some one to God. Perhaps these are omissions that we think very little about; but he thought much about them. He thought them matters of self-accusation.

We will take another Saint, a Bishop in England —S. Thomas of Hereford—a most fervent pastor, a man who lived a whole life of apostolic labour, 'spending and being spent' for the sake of his flock. When he was on his deathbed, his chaplains, who were round about him, said, 'My lord, would you not like to go to confession?' and he looked at them and said, 'Foolish men.' After a little pause they said again, 'Do you not know that your time is drawing near? The leech says you cannot live much longer. Would you not like to see the confessor?' He said, 'Foolish men.' A third time they said the same thing: 'The time must be near; would you not desire to make your peace with God?' And a third time he made the same answer; and so he died. Afterwards it was found that he went to confession every day. He had no need of their counsel; but he had no will to reveal what had been the habit of his life.

There is one more light in which we shall learn to know ourselves, and that is, the light of the Sacred Heart of our Divine Master. The Sacred Heart has three relations—its relation towards God, its relation towards mankind at large, and its relation towards each one of us personally. Let us set that before us and make examination of ourselves. The relation of the Heart of Jesus towards His Heavenly Father—what piety, what love, what fervour, what self-forgetfulness, what self-denial, what self-sacrifice. What is there in you corresponding to this? Alas, what is there in us? Again, the relation of the Sacred Heart of Jesus to mankind. What charity, what forgiveness, what generosity, what pity, what compassion, what intercession. What is there in us towards our neighbour like this? Thirdly, the relation of the Sacred Heart of Jesus towards ourselves personally. What tenderness, what long-suffering, what exquisite kindness, what delicate forbearance, what hopefulness, that, being such as we are, full of sins as we know, and as He knows better than we, even to this day He has borne with us; and He has not 'broken the bruised reed, nor quenched the smoking flax.' Let us compare this with ourselves, and see whether we can stand this test, and we shall learn to know ourselves.

5. And then, lastly, if any one desires to preserve his baptismal grace, he must be a man of prayer. A man without prayer is dead before God. If he does not live in union with God, speaking with God, conversing with God, depend upon it there can be little union of love between God and him. There may be

faith that God exists, and there may be a hope that some day he may begin to pray; but union of charity between God and a prayerless soul there cannot be. It is by prayer that we appreciate what God is. When the heart ascends by the intellect to the knowledge of God, when it ascends by the affections to the love of God, and when it ascends by the will to the resolution of holding fast by God, then we begin to realise that God is above all things, and worthy of all love and adoration, and that it were better for a man to lose the whole world than to lose the vision of God in eternity. And this is to be learnt in prayer, and in prayer only. The man that prays realises also the relation of God to himself as a father, and the personal relation of Jesus Christ to him as a kinsman and a brother and a friend. And, further, by the light of prayer and contemplation of God and of the Sacred Heart of Jesus, a man is 'changed into the same likeness from glory to glory, as by the Spirit of the Lord.'

We know that friends who love one another become like to each other; they catch the very tones of each other's voices; they exchange the very look of each other's countenances—features the most dissimilar acquire a strange likeness in expression. So it is with our souls, if we live in the habit of prayer;

that is, of conversing and of speaking with our Divine Friend. When Stephen stood before the council, his face shone like the face of an angel. The light of the presence of his Master in heaven fell upon it. And they who live a life of prayer are being ever changed into the likeness of their Divine Lord. I do not mean that they are outwardly transformed; I do not mean that there come rays out of their hands or their side, or that there is any resplendent light upon their countenances; but I mean this, that there is a gentleness, a sweetness, a kindness, a lowliness, an attraction about their life which makes everybody at peace with them. Everybody draws near to them with a tranquil confidence and a rest of heart. We know that with some people, though they are good and just, yet when we approach them we have a sense of fear; but where there is in any man a likeness to the Sacred Heart of Jesus there is an attraction which goes out from him. As our Divine Master said: 'I, if I be lifted up from the earth, will draw all things unto Me;' so He communicates to His servants, who are like Him, the same power of attracting others. The world calls it fascination; but what the world calls fascination is simply this, that in the measure in which men have the likeness of the Sacred Heart of Jesus, they draw others to themselves.

Just as He would draw men unto Himself if He were visible now, they do it in His stead. And there is a special strength and calm and sweetness in such characters, a sweetness which everybody feels—not simply in their charity, but in the finer influences of their charity, of charity carried into the least things, into the delicate consideration of what is due to others; not only of what is just to them, but what is equitable; not only what ought to be done in such a case, but what would be the best, the highest, the most generous, and the noblest thing to do. And the bearing of such men is calm, because they are never thrown off their balance; they live in the Divine Presence, and they neither fear anything nor court anything. The world cannot bribe them; the world cannot terrify them. And because they are independent of the world, they are inflexible; they have a gift of strength and of fortitude, and they leave their impression upon everybody around them, and they take their impressions from no one but from their Divine Master.

Now here, in outline and very insufficiently, is the way in which we, if we were faithful, might be continually growing into the likeness of our Divine Lord. If by fidelity to our baptismal grace, by good confession, by avoiding the occasions of sins which taint the soul, by growing in self-knowledge, and by living a life of prayer—if we would only so hold fast by the Sacred Heart, then assuredly God, on His part, would perpetually transform us into the same image by His Spirit of Grace.

I cannot help saying one word more of warning to parents. If these things be so, what, in the Name of God, are some parents doing, who are ready to give over their children to secular instruction and secular schools? Their first and chief aim is the cultivation of the intellect, and their last thought is the training and formation of the spiritual and moral life. These are the fathers and mothers who are wrecking the baptismal innocence of their offspring. They who ought to be guarding it are they who, of their own folly, are exposing it to every peril. They who ought to be sheltering their children in innocence and ignorance of evils which ought never to cross their soul are they who are exposing them to temptation all the day long. I can but say this in passing. The subject is too great to go into it now; it needs an ampler time. Therefore I beseech you who have any influence either over children or over parents, or over education in any form, never to depart from the great line and law of Christian education, namely, that the education of a child born again in the Sacrament of Baptism is the building up of God's spiritual work in the soul. You are called to be fellow-workers with God in the transforming of your children into the image of the Sacred Heart of Jesus.

I might also have added how precious life is, if only from our infancy we had all been faithful, if only from our childhood we had persevered in the brightness and freshness of grace in which the Holy Ghost planted us at the font. If now, in the vigour and strength of our manhood, or in the maturity of our older years, we were, not only what we are by the experience of life, but also that which we were in the innocence of our early childhood, we should be nearer to the Sacred Heart, weak and sinful as we may be. Nevertheless, see 'how great a charity our Heavenly Father hath bestowed upon us, that we should be called and should be the sons of God. Therefore the world knoweth us not, because it knew Him not. Beloved, now are we the sons of God, and it doth not yet appear what we shall be; but we know that when He shall appear we shall be like Him, and we shall see Him as He is.'[6]

[6] S. John iii. 1, 2.

IX.

THE SIGNS OF THE SACRED HEART.

THE SIGNS OF THE SACRED HEART.

If our heart reprehend us not, then we have confidence towards God. Dearly beloved, if our heart reprehend us, God is greater than our heart, and knoweth all things. 1 S. JOHN iii. 20, 21.

WE have already seen in what conformity consists. S. Paul, writing to the Romans, says, 'Be not conformed to this world, but be ye reformed in the newness of your minds;' that is to say, 'Put off the world, for they that love the world are at enmity with God: be reformed, made over again, recreated, become new creatures.' Our reformation is nothing less than a new creation; and conformity consists, as we have seen, chiefly in humility, which lays the axe to the root of our pride; and in charity, which quenches our natural anger; and in forgetfulness of self, which is the direct contrary to the passion that governs most men—the love of self. We have also considered the means whereby this transformation into conformity is to be effected; and we saw, as you will remember, that these means consist in a steady and constant fidelity to our baptismal grace; secondly, if we depart from it, in good confession; thirdly, in avoiding the occasions of sin; fourthly, in a true knowledge of ourselves; and lastly, in a habit and spirit of prayer.

We come now to our third subject, namely, to the signs or the marks whereby we may know whether this transformation is being wrought in us or not. It is very necessary that we should know what are the certain explicit marks of this change, because we are all of us in danger of self-deception. There is not, perhaps, one of us who does not think of himself more than he deserves before God; there is not one of us who is not in danger of self-love, and self-love paints for itself all manner of pleasant pictures: and what we paint we believe ourselves to be. We set before our minds, by a sort of intellectual simulation—that is, by a creative imagination of our own, out of the lives of Saints and out of our own desires —a vision of what we wish to be, and then sometimes we straightway think that we have attained it. We have need to stand in awe of ourselves; and when S. John said, 'If our heart condemn us, God is greater than our heart, and knoweth all things,' he means to tell us that there is a higher judge more discerning, more just than we are, who is always searching us. We, in our partiality, are continually absolving ourselves when we do not deserve absolution, and continually commending ourselves when we deserve blame. 'If our heart reprehend us not, then we have confidence,' and only then; and yet God sees what we do not; for we know that Satan can change himself into an angel of light, and he can even deceive us into believing that we are invested with a multitude of graces which we do not possess; that we have beautiful and luminous characters to which we bear no likeness. Many a tree has exuberant foliage and spreads its branches heavy with leaves, but there is not a fruit to be found upon it; you all remember the barren fig-tree. Therefore we have need to fix upon some certain test by which to examine ourselves. S. John by the word 'heart' means our conscience; for our conscience is made up of our intellect judging of right and wrong, and our moral sense approving or condemning: it is therefore a united intellectual and moral act. The intellect sitting as a moral judge is the conscience; and the conscience is the heart, because it passes sentence, a moral sentence following upon the judgment of the intellect; both act as one tribunal with a concurrent jurisdiction: and therefore here the word 'heart' signifies emphatically the conscience, but it means also the whole soul. If our soul condemn us not by our inward spiritual consciousness, then we have confidence towards God.

Now, first of all, it is clear that whosoever knowingly commits any deliberate sin has the mark of deformity upon him. If we had the deliberate choice offered to us of committing a mortal sin against God or of dying on the spot, we ought, without a moment's doubt, to choose rather to die than to sin mortally; for to die is only the death of the body, but mortal sin is the death of the soul. Any man who has not reached that point certainly has no mark whatsoever of conformity to the Sacred Heart of Jesus. He has the first great mark of conformity to Satan. Next, if the choice were offered to us of committing deliberately even a venial sin, we ought to suffer any pain or any loss in this world rather than commit it. We can have but little hatred of sin, but little love of God, and but little sense of gratitude if we would not readily choose to suffer anything rather than deliberately to sin against God, even though it be only by a venial sin. S. John says in this same epistle, 'Whosoever is born of God committeth not sin, for His seed abideth in him, and he cannot sin because he is born of God.'[1] When he says 'he cannot sin,'

[1] 1 S. John iii. 9.

he does not mean that it is a physical impossibility, that his free will has not the power; but it means that his moral being is so changed, so renewed, so conformed to the will of God, that to sin would violate his own new nature. It would be an outrage to his own will; it would violate his own higher and better self if he were to commit an act contrary to the will of God, with whose will his own is identified. We will now go on to the marks by which to judge ourselves.

It is clear that the signs we are to look for are not external signs, but internal altogether.

1. And the first sign is denial of self. Lest I should seem to use language which sounds too large, I will not say mortification of self, but I will say self-denial. Every man acknowledges—every one who leads the simplest, I was going to say the lowest, life that deserves to be called Christian—acknowledges the duty of self-denial. S. Paul so draws our Lord's character—'Christ did not please Himself.'[2] And this is the first sign of our being transformed into the likeness of the Sacred Heart. If a man were to work miracles, that would not suffice; for, as our Lord has said, Many shall come in that day, and say, Lord, Lord, in Thy name we have cast out devils, and

[2] Rom. xv. 3.

done many mighty works ; and He will say, Depart from Me ; I never knew you. And if a man were to do all manner of splendid works and succeed in vast enterprises which the world counts to be for the glory of God, it is not enough ; for we know the fate of those who go round about land and sea to make one proselyte, and when he is made he is twofold more the child of hell than themselves.[3] Neither, again, are long prayers a certain evidence, for the Pharisees made prayers longer than yours : nor, again, knowledge, nor alms-giving, because S. Paul says that all these things, and even martyrdom itself, without the love of God, are nothing. Neither, finally, are mortifications, such as fastings, disciplines, watchings, and the like ; all these are also nothing before God, unless there be a true inward denial of self—a mortification of the intellect and heart and will. You remember the vision of S. Antony. The tempter came to him and said, ' Antony, you fast a great deal, but I never eat ; you watch, but I never sleep ; you mortify the body, but I have no body to mortify : but you do one thing I cannot—I cannot obey.' Therefore the denial of our own will is the first sure test. Now men may be classed in three ways, and no one can escape this classification : either they

<hr>

[3] S. Matt. xxiii. 15. .

are self-pleasers, or they are men-pleasers, or they are pleasers of God. In one of these three every man will find himself. As for being self-pleasers, it means this: that we have our own will as our motive, and our own liking as our law. As for being men-pleasers, it is only another form of pleasing ourselves. It is for interest, or for pleasure, or for gain, or for honour, or for some other personal purpose that we seek to please men. But to be pleasers of God simply means that we take the example of our Divine Lord as our model. 'Christ did not please Himself;' that is to say, every act of His life was done for a higher, purer, nobler motive, and, whether it pleased self or not, was His last thought. All things high and pure and noble pleased the Sacred Heart, but it was not for that cause that He did these things. If I were to give examples, the subject of self-denial would be inexhaustible. You have the opportunity in your daily life of denying your own will. All the day long you have opportunities without number: first of all, denying yourselves for the sake of others; giving up your own will to theirs; preferring them before yourselves; giving them the first place, serving them, and asking nothing in return; exacting nothing for what costs you most; doing it in silence, and never speaking of what you have done. If you will do these things for human friends, you will promptly deny yourselves whenever you see anything that you can do, even if it be at some cost to yourselves, for the honour and the glory of God. There is no mistake about this test. In itself it is unpalatable to nature; and no man goes against his own will for the sake of pleasing himself. He has a higher motive—the love of the Sacred Heart and desire of conformity to his Master.

2. Secondly, another sign in which we cannot be mistaken is charity towards others. The whole perfection of man in time and in eternity is made up of charity to God and to our neighbour. Eternal bliss by union with God is charity. Now by charity I do not mean giving alms, and I do not mean giving bread to the hungry, drink to the thirsty, and the like; all that is a part of the law of nature; mere humanity prompts it and demands it.

The charity of the spiritual order is a divine character. Let us take it in examples. First, there is charity towards the sins of others. If we see anything which our heart would condemn in ourselves, before we condemn others let us think what perhaps may have been their childhood, their education, their opportunities, their privations; let us think also what may have been their temptations, how things which in us would be sins, in them perhaps, from want of light, may be hardly faults. Once more: we must charitably judge of their intentions, of what they mean, knowing that the will and the deed are the same. Let us also charitably consider their follies, and not burst out like a flame, as we often do, at the foolish conduct of others. The Sacred Heart bears with our follies, and they are many. Let us be charitable also to their falls, remembering that we stand by the help of God, and by that alone. 'By the grace of God I am that which I am.' In the sight of God we may be more guilty than they. When our Divine Lord was upon earth, He was surrounded all the day long by sinners—sinners on every side, sinners of every kind, sinners in every degree;. and yet He bore with them with a sweetness, a patience, and a gentleness which were never exhausted, never ruffled. He was even reproached for His lenity, as if He were indifferent to sin. He was called 'the friend of sinners;' as if He loved their society. 'This man receiveth sinners, and eateth with them;' as if He sought them by His own choice. But He 'pleased not Himself.' Nor did He suffer among sinners only. In the midst of His disciples, of those who came to Him as His friends, what follies, what faults, what contentions, what jealousies, what wearisome misunderstandings; and yet He bore them all. He was surrounded by His chosen Apostles, whom He had selected to be nearest to Himself, and whom He destined to be most like Himself; and yet what contentions, what rivalries, what ambitions, what self-seeking, what indignation against each other, what misconceptions of His words, what slowness to believe; yet how He bore with all their imperfections. We never hear a word of sharp reproof out of His mouth, never a word of hasty condemnation. This is the patient love of the Sacred Heart; and unless we are somewhat like it in this, be it ever so little, the work of transformation cannot be far advanced in us.

3. And then, thirdly, there is only one person in the world to whom we may be severe. There is one who deserves it, and we may vent all our severity on that person, and that person is.our own self. A sure token of a charitable heart will be that a man is gentle to everybody, but unsparing to himself; that is to say, he will remember that there is nobody whom he knows to have committed more sins than he knows of himself. Why, I ask you, did S. Paul say that he was 'the chief of sinners'? He was not using exaggeration, neither was he speaking rhetorically. He did not mean to deceive anybody; he meant what

he said; and what, then, did he mean?   He meant
this: 'I know my own consciousness from my childhood to this day; and the history of my past is upon
me as far and as fully as my memory reaches, and
that knowledge is next to the knowledge that God
has of me.   I know therefore there is no one that I
know as I know myself, and no man knows me as I
know myself; and though I may see other men
commit many sins, yet I never see any man commit
so many as I can number in myself when I go back
to the beginning of my life and look over my boyhood, youth, and manhood, running down to the present moment.   I can see sins of commission, sins of
omission, venial sins, alas, perhaps mortal too.   I
see there a long reckoning which I can number and
count up, and I cannot number or count up the same
amount of sins in any other man.   And, next, I
know nobody who has received so many graces of the
Holy Spirit as God in His goodness has bestowed
upon me.   I was struck down on the way to Damascus when I was bent on persecuting the disciples of
Jesus; I was converted in the midst of my sins, by
a miracle of grace, by a vision of my Divine Saviour, and by the power of the Holy Ghost; and I
know nobody that has ever had a grace so great nor
a conversion so miraculous.   And if, after such a

s

miracle of grace as that, I am what I am, and what
I know myself to be, certainly I know of no one
more sinful, no one who has received such tokens of
God's love, and who has done so little in return.'   If
you remember how many are the gifts and the graces
of the Holy Spirit which you have received ever since
your baptism,—how abundantly and how generously
God has dealt with you ; how He has shown you the
light of His Truth, and has drawn you by the attraction of His Love, and has striven to bring you to Himself ; and how often you have resisted, how often you
have gone out of the way, how often you have turned
a blind eye and a deaf ear ; how often you have taken
your hand from the plough, how often you have
turned back again ; with what languid and lingering
steps you have returned, and how little heart you had
to go back to God—what little use you have made of
all those graces—if you cast up this great account,
and set on one side the mercies of God to you, and on
the other the abuse of His gifts and the little profit
and advancement you have made, I think there is
not one of us that will not say, 'I see a great many
sinners round about me ; I see a great many who
have done more glaring and open sins than I have ;
but I must confess that, though there is many a man
who may have committed more grievous material

sins than I have, yet I know of no sins which have been committed with the formal sinfulness that I know in myself. And, therefore, I can say with truth, " sinners of whom I am chief." ' This is what the Apostle meant, and this is what every one of us must also say. Well, then, if we so know ourselves, we shall most assuredly be severe to nobody else. The parable of the Pharisee and the publican teaches us that lesson. The Pharisee did not know himself, and he stood by himself in the temple, and looked upon the poor publican afar off. The Pharisee went boldly into the temple; the poor publican standing at a distance would not so much as lift up his eyes; and the Pharisee said, ' God, I thank Thee that I am not as other men are, nor even as this publican. I give tithes of all that I possess, I fast twice in the week;' and so on. And the other beat upon his breast and said, ' God, be merciful to me a sinner.' And of the two, which went down to his house justified; that is, forgiven, absolved, and at peace with God ? Once more. You will remember when our Divine Saviour sat at the table of Simon the Pharisee. Simon was a just man. There is no reason to believe that this Pharisee was other than a man who lived in the fear of God and literally kept His commandments; but he was a man whose charity was small and whose severity was great, and both were expressed. His charity was for himself, and his severity was for his neighbour. In this case his severity fell upon the Son of God, and he said, ' This man, if He were a prophet, would have known who and what manner of woman this is that touches Him;' and he condemned Him in his heart. Let this be a warning. If we have charity to others, the severity will be upon ourselves; we shall never spare our own faults. We shall remember the words, ' Judge not, that ye be not judged;' and ' Why say to your neighbour, Let me pull out the mote that is in thine eye, and seest not the beam that is in thine own eye?' and ' He shall have judgment without mercy who has shown no mercy; for mercy shall rejoice against judgment.'

4. Another test is a mistrust of ourselves. There is no more dangerous fault than trust in self, when any one thinks he may do whatsoever he will, go wherever he likes, see whatever he chooses, lay down the law for himself, have no fear of temptation, and no care to avoid the occasions of sin. Such a man says, ' I can trust myself. I know where I go, I know what I do; I can take care of myself, or God will take care of me;' forgetting that we say every day of our lives, ' Lead us not into tempation; but deliver us from evil;' that is to say, ' We will take care, as far as we can,

not to go into the temptation; but do Thou, Lord, watch over us and keep us from all evil.' No man can hope that he will be kept by a divine protection if he does not watch over himself. All this is self-trust. Now what is self-mistrust? It is a great fear of our own will, and a great trust in God alone. It is the consciousness that without Him we can do nothing; that without God we cannot stand; that without God we should do all evil. We ought to remember what we were when we were born into this world—spiritually dead; and after we had received the grace of Baptism, what we made ourselves again. Each one who will remember his own history, and will then ask himself, 'What am I now?' will answer, 'I am at best only half transformed into the image of my Saviour, and I am therefore still half deformed in the sight of God—half conformed and half deformed, a mixture of good and evil. As I am half conformed I see myself, and I desire to do right; and as I am half deformed, I am blind and very weak, and therefore what should I be at this moment if God had not kept me from ruining myself?' S. Philip used to say, 'Keep Thy hand upon me, put Thy hand upon my head; for if Thou shouldst let me go, I should do Thee all manner of harm.' Our only trust is in the keeping of God, in that influx of the power of God by which we live and move and are ; and in the support of the grace of God, by which alone we can do good and can avoid evil for a moment.   Therefore the Apostle says, 'Let him that thinketh himself to stand take heed lest he fall.'[4]   Wheresoever there is this mistrust of self, there will always be found, as I said before, great charity to others, and a very great care and love for the souls of sinners, with a great desire to work for our Divine Lord in their salvation.

5. And lastly—for I will give only one more test —where there is a conformity to the Sacred Heart of our Lord, there will be a spirit of praise.   The spirit of praise and the spirit of prayer ought to go to- gether.   But nothing is more certain than that we pray very often and that we praise but very seldom. We pray because we know our wants—hunger and thirst and sorrow and trouble will drive us to pray ; and when we have received the answers to our prayers, we go our way without thanking the Giver. And yet the whole of our eternity will be made up of praise, for there there will be no more prayer ; and if we do not begin to learn the spirit of praise in this world, how shall we praise God in eternity ? If we are not now in harmony with the praise which goes up before the Throne, how can we be meet for

[4] 1 Cor. x. 12.

the inheritance of the Kingdom of God? Are we even in harmony with the servants of God upon earth—I will not say with the Apostles and with the Saints of the Christian law, but with the servants of God under the old law? Take the Book of Psalms: what is it from beginning to end but one continual voice of praise to God for His goodness? And in what does praise consist? It consists in acts of love and contemplation, of joy and thanksgiving. How often do we make these acts in our devotions? And have we not matter enough for them? For instance: for the multitude of our graces, for our very existence, for our prolonged existence after our many sins, for the image of God that is in us, for the continued power of knowing and of loving Him. We were made to be the children of God, and He has bowed down, as it were, to take up our manhood that He might make us the friends of God; and yet we do not praise Him. We have to thank Him for our redemption, for the Most Precious Blood that was shed for us, for the coming and the infusion of the Holy Ghost, for the perpetual inspirations of grace, for the whole tissue and chain of our spiritual and supernatural life. We have also to thank Him for our salvation, one by one personally; that is, for the redemption applied to ourselves.

The most potent medicine which infallibly heals will heal nobody unless it be applied. If the Precious Blood be not applied to us, we shall not be cleansed; but it has been applied to us, without our seeking, in our Baptism. It has been renewed to us in our absolutions; it has been sprinkled upon us all the day long when we have made acts of true contrition. For all these things we owe Him continual praise. Can we be conscious of our own sinfulness, of our unprofitableness, of our unworthiness, of our nothingness before Him, and that we are yet His children and heirs of His Kingdom: and that He assists and preserves us from year to year and from day to day, so that we can say, 'By the grace of God I am that which I am,' and still be silent and without a word of praise? *Omnis spiritus laudet Dominum.*

Here, then, are five signs; and if we can find them, at least in their beginnings, 'our heart will not reprehend us, and we may have confidence with God.' Let us search for them in our hearts. The first is self-denial, the second is charity to others, the third is severity to ourselves, the fourth is self-mistrust, and the fifth is the spirit of praise. Where these are there is at least a faint outline of our Divine Master.

And now I will only add two plain counsels, and

the first is this : Take nothing lower than the Heart of our Divine Lord as the measure and the rule of your own. Do not take any lower standard. Do not take the examples of men. Do not take maxims or motives of your own imagining. Set before you the Sacred Heart in its full and divine perfection. The Word of God took that Sacred Heart in order that we might know God; that He might come within the sphere of our intelligence, within the reach of our hearts, and unite our will to His will. Therefore let us first of all see whether our intelligence, our reason, our intellect be conformed to the intelligence of Jesus Christ. His intelligence was, like our own, a human and finite intelligence. He had also an infinite intelligence; therefore He said, 'I am the Truth.' And how are we to know this truth? He has revealed it. And where is that revelation? In the holy faith. Any man who knows only a part of that revelation, that is, only a fragment, or any number of fragments of that revelation, has not his reason nor his intelligence conformed to the reason and intelligence of Jesus Christ. He is narrowed in some part. But when his whole understanding and reason are illuminated by the knowledge of faith, then he is conformed to the intelligence of Jesus Christ; the whole outline, and I will say the whole circle, of his reason is full of light. We must, then, be perfect in the light of Catholic faith. Next as to our affections. The Sacred Heart is the most perfect Kingdom of God the Father. It is the sanctuary in which God the Son perpetually dwells, and it is also the most perfect work of the Holy Ghost. All the affections and all those pro-passions, as they are called—because the Church never speaks of passions when it speaks of the Sacred Heart—all the emotions, all those sensitive movements of our nature which were in Him, were all in perfect tranquillity, in perfect order, and in perfect unity. Therefore until our sensitive will, with all its affections and emotions, is subject to our superior will, which is our reason and our conscience, and until both the sensitive and the superior will in us are subject to the will of God, we shall not be conformed to the Sacred Heart of our Lord. And, once more, His will is the law of ours; and unless our will be conformed to our lot in life; unless we accept it as coming from the will of God; unless our will accepts our state in life, and does not chafe against it, because God in His providence has ordained it for us—I will even go further, and say, unless we accept our state in grace as God has given it to us— we shall not be conformed to Him. Many people are all day long complaining and chafing that they fall into faults. True, indeed, they do; and why? They are impatient to be Saints for their own glory, or to be masters of themselves for their own consolation, or to be perfectly sanctified with all speed, that they may be delivered from the trouble of mortifying themselves; and God in His wisdom measures out to them the grace which He sees to be sufficient for them if they are faithful; and by leaving them long in that warfare He humbles them, by teaching them to know themselves; and He makes the very sins which they once loved to be their chastisement, and to scourge them for those very faults. He turns their faults into a purgatory upon earth, and by suffering from them they are purified, and make their expiation. Until we have come to say even in this what our Lord said in the garden, 'Not my will but Thine be done,' we are not conformed to the Sacred Heart. When we can say it, then we may hope that our affections and our intelligence and our will are growing towards His likeness.

And the other counsel is this: Do not be cast down if, when you look into yourselves, you find your heart to be so deformed, so unlike to the Sacred Heart of Jesus. Anybody who really knows himself will find in his own heart what we read in the beginning, 'a great deep,' and 'darkness on the face of the deep'—that is, a disorder and a confusion—but over all the Spirit of God moves 'upon the face of the waters.' There is much in ourselves that we have never fathomed. The darkness hides much from ourselves. And the more we know ourselves the more at first we must be cast down and troubled, so as even to be altogether out of heart if we did not know that the more we are humbled before God the more safe we are, and the more surely His Presence is in us. If we find in ourselves all manner of windings and doubles, and that the heart is deceitful above all things, who shows all this to us? who teaches us these truths? It is the Spirit of God moving over our inward life, and by His light revealing us to our own selves. Therefore, when we come to see these things, we have no reason to be cast down; it is the evidence and the certain proof that God is working in us of His own good will. And the way in which He works is this. When the Holy Spirit of God comes into the heart of a man, He enlightens him to know himself, but the Spirit of God is invisible; while He is showing ourselves to our own conscience He hides Himself. And when He casts His light upon us, He shows to us, not the things that are pleasing to us, but the things that are displeasing to Him ; not those things which will please our love of self, but those things which will displease and humble us. He does not show the conformity, if we have any, to the Sacred Heart, but the manifold deformities which are displeasing in God's sight.

But perhaps you will say, 'How can I ever be conformed to the Sacred Heart of Jesus?' You can never transform yourselves into His likeness; but there is One who can; there is One who will transform you by His creating power. If you go to Him that made you, He can make all things new. Old things will pass away. If you say, 'Create in me a clean heart'—that is, 'Put forth Thine almighty power to make me once more as Thou didst make me in the beginning'—He will renew His own work. 'If any man be in Christ Jesus, he is a new creature.' His work is not by halves, nor upon the surface, nor left imperfect, like something which is just refitted for the time, or made up again like new cloth on an old garment. It is a new creation, made over again—'a new creation, in which old things are passed away and all things are become new.' 'He that sitteth upon the Throne said, Behold, I make all things new.' The Precious Blood will cleanse away all sin; though it be red as scarlet, it shall be as white as snow; though it be like crimson, it shall be as wool; the almighty power of the Holy Ghost will purify all things as ' by the spirit of burning.' He will re-create all things and make them over again. As the springing of the harvest or the putting out of the leaf in the forest is a new creation upon the stock of the old by the almighty power of God, so in body and soul and spirit you will be made new once more.

Therefore, to make what I have said very practical, and to bring it nearer home, I will say this : Follow out and pursue your little faults. If you will correct your little faults, I was going to say your great ones will correct themselves ; for ' he that is faithful in that which is least is faithful in that which is greater.' Be watchful against spiritual sins, faults of omission, sins of the tongue, and thoughts against charity. And secondly, Fulfil your little duties, and your greater ones will take heed for themselves. A man that fulfils the lesser duties of charity, of humility, of piety, of fidelity, will have a conscience that grows more and more delicate; and a delicate conscience will take care of the great commandments of God. Then your ' heart will not reprehend you,' ' and God, who is greater than your heart,' will keep you in the multitude of peace. Your many infirmities will be absolved in the Precious Blood of His Son, and if your ' heart reprehend' you ' not, then have you confidence towards God;' and as S. John goes on in this place to say, 'Whatsoever we ask of Him we shall receive, because we keep His commandments, and do those things which are pleasing in His sight.'[5]

[5] 1 S. John iii. 23.

X.

THE ETERNAL GLORY OF THE SACRED HEART.

THE ETERNAL GLORY OF THE SACRED HEART.

The glory which Thou hast given Me I have given to them.
S. John xvii. 22.

We have now reached the end of our thoughts about the glories of the Sacred Heart. We have seen it in His Incarnation, on which even the angels desire to look and cannot fathom. We have seen it in its radiance, which pervades the intellect and the heart by faith and love; and in the manifold glories of His Presence in the Sacrament of the Altar; and in the transformation of the world and the reign of His Vicar over the kingdoms of men, by which He conforms them to His own will. Such are His glories in the order and time of grace. But there still remains the eternal glory of the Sacred Heart, when time shall be no more, and the elect shall be gathered, and the divine judgment shall have winnowed the world, and the heavenly court shall rest for ever in the vision of peace. Then shall all the blessed share in His glory.

The glory of the Incarnate Son of God is twofold. He has the glory of God the Father, being consubstantial with Him, and He has His own glory as Redeemer of the world. The eternal glory of God is His by right. He is 'the brightness of His Father's glory.' The essential glory of the Ever-blessed Trinity is common to the Three coequal Persons. But He has also the glory of the Incarnation, by which He redeemed the world. S. John says, 'We beheld His glory, the glory as of the Only-begotten of the Father.' But this is the glory of the Sacred Humanity of Jesus. His glory, therefore, is both infinite and finite, essential and accidental; and both unite in one Person, and are both alike His.

Now it is of this glory that our Lord spoke when He said, ' The glory which Thou hast given Me I have given to them.' All that is communicable of His glory He has given to us; and our glory will flow for ever from the eternal fountain of His divine glory which, being uncreated, He cannot give to any creature.

The first glory that He has given to us is the gift of adoption. ' The Son of God was made Man that men might be made the sons of God;' by communication of His deified humanity to us, and by conformity to Himself. And this gift was bestowed upon us in our regeneration, by the infusion of the

Holy Ghost. The superadded gift of the Spirit, which is not due to our manhood, nor is contained within its limits, but was, of God's free and sovereign grace, given, over and above the natural perfections of our humanity to Adam, is now in a measure, and with the penalties of the Fall still attaching to us, given to all who are born again of water and of the Holy Ghost.

And what is begun in our regeneration is ever growing as we are transformed into the likeness of our Divine Lord; and this transformation is crowned and sealed in the perfect conformity of our whole humanity, glorified in soul and body, in the day when we shall see Him as He is. Then will be accomplished the work of the new creation, of Him who sitteth upon the throne, saying, 'Behold, I make all things new.'[1] 'If any be in Christ he is a new creature: the old things are passed away; behold, all things are become new.'[2] The old creation, with all its wounds and darkness and turbulence, will be gone for ever, and the new creation will be revealed in the resurrection by the glory of the sons of God. 'The first Adam was made into a living soul, the last Adam into a quickening spirit.'[3] 'The first man was of the earth, earthly; the second

[1] Apoc. xxi. 5. [2] 2 Cor. v. 17. [3] 1 Cor. xv. 45.

Man from heaven, heavenly.' 'As in Adam all die, so also in Christ all shall be made alive. But every one in his own order: the firstfruits Christ; then they that are Christ's, who have believed in His coming. Afterwards the end, when He shall have delivered up the kingdom to God and the Father, when He shall have brought to naught all principality and power and virtue. For He must reign until He hath put all enemies under His feet.' 'And when all things shall be subdued unto Him, then the Son also Himself shall be subject unto Him that put all things under Him, that God may be all in all.'[4]

The temporal reign of the Son will then be accomplished. This dead world and all its elements will be dissolved with burning heat. The new heaven and the new earth will be revealed. The Mystical Body will be gathered from warfare on earth, and from expiation in Purgatory, into the Paradise of God. All will be consummated; the number of the elect will be full; the last saint, the last penitent will have been gathered by the angels from the four winds of heaven. All will then be sealed with an eternal conformity to the Sacred Heart. And in that day, between Him and us there will be no veil for ever: our

---

[4] 1 Cor. xv. 22-28.

eyes will be no more 'holden that we cannot know Him.' They will be opened in that day when He shall drink the fruit of the Vine new with us in the Kingdom of God. We shall not then break any more the Bread of life in Sacraments; but we shall see Him, the Substance and the Reality, the Word Incarnate, the King in His beauty; and to all eternity we shall behold Him, and by and through Him we shall see God. The Sacrament of the Altar will be transfigured into the presence, real, personal, and visible, of Jesus upon the throne of His glory. The tabernacle of God in heaven will be open, and we shall see Him, with the piercing intuition of the light of glory; for to the glorified intelligence all is transparent and luminous, as the light of noon. There will be seen, with open face and for ever, all that we believe in now—the eternal glory of the Sacred Heart, the Object of our divine worship, the Original to which we are made, the Fountain of eternal life.

We will, then, end our thoughts about the Sacred Heart by contemplating its eternal glory in the midst of the hierarchies of heaven, encompassed by the multitude which no man can number of the blessed in eternal peace. In what will this glory consist? So far as we can understand, it will be revealed in three ways: first, in itself; secondly, in its relations to the Ever-blessed Trinity; and lastly, in its relations to us.

1. Let us first take its glory in itself. This also will consist of three things, which we believe here, but the blessed will see and understand in the Kingdom of God. First, the Sacred Heart is the purest of all God's created works. When He made all things in the beginning, He made them very good. The dust or the slime of the earth was holy and pure, and of it He made the first Adam. The humanity and the heart of the first Adam had no taint, nor shadow of taint of sin. Yet it was of the earth, earthy. Man was made a little lower than the angels, because he was clothed in a body of dust. Yet the heart of Adam was without sin, and perfect in itself. But the Heart of the Second Adam was taken from the substance of a sinless Mother, who, by a special privilege of the Holy Ghost, had been herself exempted from the law of sin, which had wrecked the world; her substance had been sanctified and invested by the Holy Ghost from the first moment of her existence. Grace anticipated nature, and the Holy Ghost excluded its approach. The substance of the Sacred Heart was therefore taken of a substance already sanctified, and not only exempted from the taint of sin, but elevated above

the common lot of creatures by an immaculate conception and a special relation to the Ever-blessed Trinity. She was already, in the predestination of God, the elect daughter of the Eternal Father, the Mother of the Son, the Spouse of the Holy Ghost. The Body of Jesus is therefore in its substance and structure and symmetry—the very flesh and blood, with all the wonderful organisation and properties of our humanity—the purest, noblest, and most perfect that the Creator ever wrought for His own glory. When the lance pierced it, the most delicate and elaborate work of divine wisdom and power was wrecked. When the stateliness and structure of a lily are crushed, all its beauty and perfection are revealed by contrast with its ruin; when the side of Jesus was opened, the Heart of the Man of Sorrows, the Heart that wept in Bethany and yearned over Jerusalem, revealed all its love.

This Heart, with all its most precious Blood, hypostatically united in its assumption to the Person of the Eternal Word, is the most perfect work of the new creation, and the new creation is the most perfect work of the almighty wisdom of God.

But further: this deified Heart of our manhood was quickened and animated by the most perfect soul that ever proceeded out of the will of God. In

the order of the Incarnation—not of time but **of**
reason—the Eternal Son assumed this human soul
by uniting Himself with its intelligence, and thereby
also with its love and with its will. The divine nature
assumed our manhood by that part of its perfection
which is nearest to God. His own image is in our
intelligence. The human soul of Jesus was in all
things like the soul of the first Adam, having affections and sympathies, and capacities of sorrow and
of bliss, with a will free and imperial to command
obedience in all its movements.

Moreover this perfect human soul was sanctified
by a twofold sanctification. It was sanctified by
union with the Person of the Eternal Word. The
uncreated sanctity of God thereby pervaded it. It
was anointed with the Godhead of the Son. For 'He
(the Christ) anointed Himself, anointing as God
with His own divinity, and (being) anointed as Man;
forasmuch as the Godhead is the unction of the
manhood.'[5] It was sanctified also by the infinite
sanctity of the Holy Ghost, which dwelt in it by
habitual grace and virtues and gifts and fruits and
beatitudes. And the Sacred Heart of Jesus is the
human heart of flesh and blood taken from His
Mother, with all its pure and perfect affections;

[5] S. John Dam. lib. iii. c. iii. *De Fid. Orthod.*

anointed by this twofold sanctification, infinite and finite, of the Eternal Son and of the Eternal Spirit. Such is and ever will be in eternity the Sacred Heart of Jesus, with all its natural, supernatural, and divine perfections; with all its purities and sanctities and glories. If 'the just shall shine forth like the sun in the Kingdom of their Father,' what shall be the splendours of the Sacred Heart? It is this that makes His throne white with a surpassing glory. In the midst of the heavenly court, at the head of the new creation, in all the abysses of its light and beauty, there will be one greater light ruling the eternal day—the Sacred Heart, resplendent with intensity of all created and uncreated glory.

2. The second glory of the Sacred Heart is in its relations to the Ever-blessed Trinity. It is the eternal bond between the uncreated and the creature. God has many kingdoms; but of all, the highest and the amplest is the Sacred Heart. From all eternity, God dwelt in His own immensity. He inhabited His own glory; and He rested in His own bliss. The mutual knowledge and love of the Father, Son, and Holy Ghost constitute the divine glory and the divine beatitude. But the charity of God willed not to be contained within the limits of His own

bliss. He, of His own free will and out of His own divine love, called into existence all orders of created things, that there might be out of Himself an object of His complacency : a friend whom He might love, by whom He might be loved again. Therefore He created man to His own likeness for His own glory and for our bliss. But even this did not suffice : it was not enough that we should exist and that He should have, out of Himself, the love of His creatures ; He willed to identify Himself with them ; He therefore took upon Him a created nature. God the Son assumed a created manhood into the unity of His Person ; and the created and the uncreated were joined together by a personal and eternal bond. The immensity of the divine nature and glory met the highest perfection of human nature in the unity of the Person of the Incarnate Word. The whole divine and uncreated glory was in contact, and more than in contact, with the whole world of created existence in one only point ; and that point of contact is the Sacred Heart of Jesus. It became, therefore, the most glorious of the kingdoms of the Eternal Father. The Father is not incarnate, but He is consubstantial with the Incarnate Son. He who inhabiteth eternity, and is present in all things that are made, rational and irrational, dwells by a special presence of love and complacency in the Sacred Heart of His Son. He reigns in it and over it. By it His will is ever obeyed; upon it His laws are written. Never was the Father so obeyed as by the Son in whom He is well pleased. Never was the Father so loved, adored, and praised as by the beatific acts of the Sacred Heart.

But it is more than the Kingdom of the Father. It is the special sanctuary in which the great High-Priest has redeemed the world. In it He for ever glorified God by a worship of infinite humility and fervour. In the moment of the Incarnation a human heart loved God with all its strength and saw God with all the intensity of beatific vision. When by the will of the Father and the co-operation of the Holy Ghost the Son assumed the vestments of His Priesthood, they assisted in vesting the great High-Priest for His eternal sacrifice. He put on our humanity as the alb and the stole of His sacerdotal office. And in that sacerdotal vesture He will stand before God for ever, assisted by those whom He has made a kingdom of priests unto the Father. But the Sacred Heart is the victim as well as the priest. He is the spotless Lamb, the Lamb that will lie to all eternity as slain upon the altar. And that altar is also the Sacred Heart, in which He is

for ever saying, 'Not My will but Thine be done.'
It is likewise the golden censer in the hands of our
great High-Priest, from which the frankincense in a
cloud of praise and thanksgiving goes up for ever
before the eternal throne.   Though, when all is fulfilled, He will no more offer sacrifice nor exercise the
priestly office, nevertheless He will be for ever the
eternal High-Priest reigning in the glory of the
new creation redeemed with His Divine Blood.[6]

But once more : the Sacred Heart will be to all
eternity the most perfect creation and the most glorious temple of the Holy Ghost.   It was ' conceived
by the Holy Ghost,' and from that instant it was
inhabited and sanctified by the Third Person of the
Holy Trinity, who not only replenished it with all
created grace, but united Himself to it by a substan-
tial union.   As in all the just the Holy Ghost
dwells not as the fragrance only of the ointment, but
as the very substance, so He dwells in fulness in
the Head of the Mystical Body, and in the Heart from
which its eternal life is derived.   The Sacred Heart
was always in the Beatific Vision in right of the
Eternal Son ; but the Soul of Jesus has also the
light of glory from the Holy Ghost,[7] with which it

<hr>

[6] Vasquez, disp. lxxxv. c. iii. 30, tom. vi. p. 577.
[7] S. Thom. p. iii. q. x. a. ii. iv.

beholds the uncreated Nature and threefold personality of God.[8]

Such, then, is the essential glory of the Sacred
Heart, in which the uncreated charity of God in
infinite perfection dwells; in which the created
charity of God is poured forth in fulness, without
measure; in an immensity which cannot be conceived.
The glory and the bliss of eternity will be measured
by charity and by the merit of every soul. What,
then, will be for ever the glory of the deified body of
Jesus and the glory of His Name, which is above
every name?[9] If one drop of the Blood of the Sacred
Heart was enough to redeem the world, it was also
enough to obtain for it an immensity of eternal glory.

Therefore the whole court of heaven to all eternity will worship the Sacred Heart, saying, 'Holy,
Holy, Holy, Lord God Almighty, who was, and who is,
and who is to come;' and they shall give 'glory and
honour and benediction to Him that sitteth upon the
throne, who liveth for ever and ever;' and 'they shall
adore Him that liveth for ever and ever, and cast
their crowns before the throne, saying, Thou art
worthy, O Lord, to receive glory and honour and

[8] Petav. *De Incarn.* lib. xi. c. iv. 8. Melchior Canus, *Loci
Theol.* lib. xiii. p. 438.

[9] Vasquez, disp. lxxix. c. i. ii. S. Thom. p. iii. q. xlix. a. vi.

power, because Thou hast created all things, and for Thy will they were and have been created.'[10]

3. But there remains yet another glory in the relations of the Sacred Heart to us. I am not speaking of what it is to us now in this state of warfare, but of what it will be to all eternity. It is now the Heart of our Kinsman, our Brother, our Friend, our Saviour, our Redeemer, of our Lord and of our God, of the Good Physician full of healing, of the Good Shepherd full of loving care. All this He is to us now in the multiplicity of our needs and in all the manifold activity of His grace. All our life long we are eliciting fresh revelations of His love : testing by experience new evidences of His sympathy, and tasting new gifts of His sweetness. What we are learning here will be known by a direct and eternal knowledge there. The Sacred Heart will be to us in the Kingdom of His glory all that it has ever been in the time of our warfare upon earth, with this only difference : what we know now in part we shall know there even as we are known ; what we have here believed there we shall see ; what we have hoped we shall enjoy ; what we have tasted as it were by drops falling like manna in the wilderness we shall then enjoy in abiding fulness. We shall rest in that land

[10] Apoc. iv. 8-11

which is now far off, in the realm of the King in His beauty. In that promised land every man shall sit down under his vine and under his fig-tree. The Sun of Bliss shall stand at eternal noon over the land of promise, in the Paradise of God. Our relations there with the Sacred Heart shall be, not as now in the twilight and variations of our infirmity, but intuitive, conscious, and changeless.

We shall gaze upon it as the centre of the heavenly court, of the hierarchy of Saints and Angels, of Thrones and Powers, of Cherubim and Seraphim, of the Mystical Body, in which shall be glorified every Saint, from Abel the just to the last who has washed his robes in the Blood of the Heart of God. Then will be revealed the mystery of that unity against which the gates of hell have never prevailed; of that indissoluble mystery of Jesus with all His members which from earth has risen to the throne of the Eternal. We shall wonder then, not that it has never perished, but that we ever were afraid.

But there is still another glory of the Sacred Heart. It is the Fountain of Life. It is the Spring-head of the River of the Water of Life. The mission of the Holy Ghost in time flows through the Incarnate Son and from His Sacred Heart. All the mysteries of the new creation, in the external operations of the Spirit in the Church, and in the internal operations of the Spirit in the soul,—all come from the Sacred Heart. ' The Spirit breatheth where He will, and thou hearest His voice ; but thou knowest not whence He cometh or whither He goeth.'[11] Nicodemus did not know, but we do know, whence He cometh. Jesus ' breathed on them, and said, Receive ye the Holy Ghost.'[12] He comes through the Word made Flesh, and therefore from the Sacred Heart. *Omnia per Cor Jesu:* all things come through the Heart of Jesus. From the beginning of the world the Lamb was slain, and the Sacred Heart was pierced. The whole flood and inundation of the Spirit which has healed the world has descended from the wound in the side of Jesus. The Water and the Blood became the rivers of salvation to Adam and to Eve and to Abel and to Enoch and to the Patriarchs, to Job in Madian, to Melchisedech king of Salem, to the tribes of Israel, to every soul in every age and in every land and tongue to whom salvation came. As every drop of the rain which softens the earth, and every ray of light that warms it, comes from the Eternal Goodness, so every grace of truth, every inspiration, every impulse, every gleam of faith, every sting of conscience, every tear of

[11] S. John iii. 8.   [12] Ib. xx. 22.

contrition, has come through the Sacred Heart. And in the glory of the Father all the blessed shall for ever see the Fountain and the Head of that great stream of life, of that mighty flood of 'the multitude of peace' and of 'the multitude of sweetness' which came down upon them here in all the manifold vicissitudes of earth, when they did not seek it and whence they did not know. How great will be the joy and the bliss in that eternal day when the tabernacle of God shall be opened, and we shall see the sanctuary out of which the waters flowed to us. We shall then share in the bliss of the Good Shepherd in the day when He is in the midst of His sheep; when His whole flock shall have been told for the last time and the number is full for all eternity ; all the lost found, and those that were dead alive for evermore. If there be joy in heaven over one sinner doing penance, what joy shall there be when all the innocent and all the penitent shall rejoice in the great harvest home, and be glorified together.

But there still remain mysteries of the Sacred Heart which here at least we shall never reach. We have but gazed upon the surface of this multitude of lights. How can it be that He who so loves all men as to die for them shall be infinitely blessed, even though He know how many are still lost? 'He who numbereth the stars and calleth them all by their names' knows every soul for whom He died, both those who are saved and those who perish. His love for the lost will yet remain, for He is immutable; but His holiness and His justice are also changeless. We cannot reason of these things. The intellect may try to square this circle, but the heart is unpersuaded. We cannot tell how the Sacred Heart can in unclouded bliss contemplate the three-and-thirty years on earth, and all the sweetness of Bethlehem and Nazareth, and Bethany and the corn-fields, and Tabor and the guest-chamber, and Emmaus and the sea of Tiberias, while Jerusalem and Calvary are not forgotten in the vivid light, not of memory but of knowledge. And so with us. In the full and personal recognition of all the blessed, how shall our bliss be perfect though many shall not be there? We cannot tell; save only that we shall be like Him, and our conformity to His Sacred Heart will make His joys and ours to be the same, and His perfect bliss will perfect ours; and in diverse measures of beatitude all will be full, and where all are full there is no pain of loss, no desire unfulfilled. And yet this is but to darken counsel with words of little understanding. *In monte Domini videbitur;* and till we are with Him in the mountain, we shall never see or understand. Then we shall intuitively see that the Sacred Heart is the source of all bliss and glory, and ' in His light we shall see light.'

The last crowning gift to us is the light of glory. No eye of flesh can see God; no intellect by the powers of nature can gaze upon the Beatific Vision. No man in the order of nature can see God and live. Even the prophet Isaias, when the glory of the Lord filled the temple, cried out in fear, ' Woe is me, . . . a man of unclean lips ; . . . and I have seen with my eyes the King, the Lord of Hosts.'[13] The first human heart that saw God was the Heart of Jesus; and in Him and through Him all His members receive a share in His divine intuition. Their intellect is elevated to the vision of God, and is likewise glorified by the light of the Holy Ghost, so as to receive a supernatural power of sight. We shall see the eternal uncreated Unity, the Essence, which is Itself, and of Itself ; the Three coequal Persons, alike in all things save only Their relations: alike in nature, wisdom, power, holiness, purity, justice, mercy : distinct in Paternity, Filiation, and Procession. And in the light of that Beatific Vision will be seen the glories of the Incarnation, of the assumption of manhood into God, of the two perfect natures in the one

---

[13] Isaias vi. 5.

only Person, God and Man—the deifying and the deified—and the relations of the Father and of the Son and of the Holy Ghost to the Sacred Heart of the Word made Flesh. How these things shall be seen God only knoweth, and they who before us have entered into the land of vision. But as the firmament and the sea and the earth, with all their glories, are visible to our eye, so the vision of God shall be seen with all its abysses of uncreated light by the glorified intelligence. We shall see God by the light of glory wholly and yet not as a whole, because of His infinity; but the Sacred Heart we shall see wholly and altogether by the intuition of love and the experience of sweetness, save only where its beauty and its glory ascend beyond the finite into the infinite, beyond the Manhood into the Godhead of Jesus, who is 'most high in the glory of God the Father.'

Such, then, very dimly and as in a glass, is the eternal glory of the Sacred Heart in its threefold relations to Itself, to the Ever-blessed Trinity, and to us; and such It will be for ever in the glory of God and of His eternal Kingdom. The heavenly city, where God shall dwell with His blessed, has no need of any light to lighten it, for the glory of God and of the Sacred Heart are the light thereof.

We can go no further. Perhaps I have already ventured too far. Into this third heaven no man can ascend; and if he were caught up into it, he could not tell the things which it is unlawful even for those who have seen them to utter. And for those who have never seen more than the faint refracted radiance of glories that are beyond the horizon of our dark world, it is better to rest in silence and holy fear and the contemplation of implicit faith.

And after looking upward into this world of light it is hardly possible, all at once, to turn back to the thoughts of penance and warfare or of the world. It is good for us to be here, not to build tabernacles of dreamy imagination, but to strengthen ourselves with a more penetrating sense of the presence of God and of our intimate relations to the Word Incarnate. The Sacred Heart in its very substance is glorified; and He has promised to change the body of our humiliation into the likeness of the body of His glory. If the body of this death in which we suffer shall then be so glorious, how ought we to watch over its sanctification now. The Precious Blood was shed for it. The very substance of our flesh and blood is therefore sacred. Every sense and every member of our body belong to the Sacred Heart. Shall I, then, take them and make them members of the world or of sin ?

The body is not for sin, 'but for the Lord, and the Lord for the body.'[14] 'He who is joined to the Lord is one spirit.' 'Know you not that your members are the temple of the Holy Ghost, who is in you, whom you have from God, and you are not your own? For you are bought with a great price. Glorify and bear God in your body.'[15] If you are saved, every hair of your head will be glorified.'

But if our body is consecrated to the Sacred Heart, how much more our hearts also. 'Blessed are the clean in heart, for they shall see God.' But no heart will be clean but such as is cleansed by watchfulness, penance, mortification, and habitual communion with the Heart of our Divine Master. Out of the heart come all evil things. But for the most part they find their way there first through the open windows of sense. The eyes and the ears and the lips and the hands and the feet are the channels by which the reason and the conscience and the memory and the heart are defiled. Lift up your eyes to the glory of the Sacred Heart in the vision of peace. Then turn inwardly upon yourselves and consecrate your hearts to Him, that every affection and desire and motive and intention and thought may be pure as He is pure.

[14] 1 Cor. vi. 13.   [15] Ib. 17, 19, 20.

The more you contemplate the glories of Jesus the more you will say or long to dare to say, 'To me to live is Christ, to die is gain.'[16] 'I have a desire to be dissolved and to be with Christ, which is a thing by far the better'[17] than the fairest, sweetest, purest, noblest happiness on earth. 'For we know that if our earthly house of this habitation be dissolved, we have a building of God, a house not made with hands, eternal in the heavens. For in this also we groan, desiring to be clothed upon with our habitation which is from heaven.' 'For we also who are in this tabernacle do groan, being burdened: because we would not be unclothed, but clothed upon, that that which is mortal may be swallowed up by life.'[18]

We are but trying to look upon the vision which the beloved disciple who lay upon the Sacred Heart alone was permitted to see.

'And he showed me a river of water of life, clear as crystal, proceeding from the throne of God and of the Lamb.' 'And there shall be no curse any more: but the throne of God and of the Lamb shall be in it, and His servants shall serve Him. And they shall see His face, and His name shall be on their foreheads.' 'I am Alpha and Omega, the First

[16] Philip. i. 21.   [17] Ib. 23.   [18] 2 Cor. v. 1, 2, 4.

and the Last, the Beginning and the End.' ' Blessed are they that wash their robes in the Blood of the Lamb.' 'I am the Root and Stock of David, the Bright and Morning Star.' 'And the Spirit and the Bride say, Come. And he that heareth, let him say, Come. And he that thirsteth, let him come : and he that will, let him take the water of life freely.'[19]

If you would find the Fountain of the Water of Life and the glories of the Eternal Throne, on which the Lord of the Sacred Heart sits and reigns for ever, go into any sanctuary where the light burns silently before the tabernacle. Kneel there and cover your face. Jesus is there, and the Ever-blessed Trinity, and the Vision of Peace, and the heavenly court, and the Kingdom of His glory.

[19] Apoc. xxii. 1, 8, 4, 13, 14, 16, 17.

INDEX.

THE END.